# Claire's Kidnapping

## SIRI HUTTON

To my lovely parents—for using *when* and not *if.*
Thank you.

# Claire

"Claire!" a holler echoed through the park.

Oh, how she knew that voice.

Picnic blankets flapped in the breeze while little children dinged the bells on their bikes as they continuously peddled about the park. The chatter from the baseball game was becoming quite noisy, but Claire had no problem getting lost in her sketches and tuning everyone and everything out. She had almost forgotten why she was there—to meet Maggie! She was glad that her friend had arrived because she was beginning to get a strange feeling from one woman nearby who seemed to have her eyes on Claire. The woman was leaning against a tree, and Claire only got to see her face as she stole a glance around the tree. Claire assumed the woman was taking a rest from her power walk. She didn't exactly want to, but she got up from the cozy, peaceful park bench to look around. Right as she popped up, her old friend finally came into view.

"Maggie!" Claire cried out while waving like a fool.

Maggie, who practically started running, slipped on a leaf, caught herself, and laughed. "I haven't seen you in ages," said the old friend, swiping at her long hair. The wind was picking up, and her face was like a magnet for her hair.

"I know! I'm surprised that we don't see each other here more often. How's life?" Claire raised an eyebrow and shifted over in her seat.

"Well, the shop keeps me busy, and . . . so does this!" Maggie replied with a grin from ear to ear while holding her hand out proudly.

A shocked expression covered Claire's face. "Oh my, congratulations!" she remarked, flabbergasted. "That's a lot of planning, isn't it?"

Engaged? She's *only* seventeen, Claire thought.

"Thank you! And oh my, yes, it is! We've already gotten as far as the date, venue, and cake! Unfortunately, I haven't been able to find a dress yet. I just really hope that I'm making the right decision!" Maggie knew she could confide in Claire with such a vulnerable concern.

"Do we ever really know one hundred percent?" Claire asked.

Maggie quickly shook her head. "We don't, do we?"

"Do you love him?"

Maggie nodded. "So much! And I want this to be my only marriage. My only love. I hope it's not that I only see the good in him and then he turns out to be a complete lunatic." Maggie giggled nervously, looking away.

"If you think this is the best decision you can make for yourself, then you should do it, Maggie. Sure, people change, but who said you can only marry someone who turns out to be a lunatic at seventeen and not twenty-seven? You are still young, we both are." Claire peered down at the leaf that fell at her feet. "I think that everyone has that bit of worry; it's just some completely call off a marriage that could have been an incredible, lifelong one because they are worried about what *could be*. So, they ruin it for themselves, even when they are completely happy."

Maggie thought for a moment, then took a breath in. "I hope you are right! About the lifelong marriage, not the lunatic!"

They both giggled like two little girls.

"I hope so too!" Claire said.

"I'm really so glad you could meet me here today." Maggie chewed on her bottom lip and fiddled with her hands. But then she sat up straighter and a smile came upon her face as she asked, "Will—will you be one of my bridesmaids?"

Claire could hardly believe that Maggie had just asked her that. Her small smile spread across her face, and her jaw dropped. "Oh, Maggie, absolutely! I'd love to!" Claire quickly wrapped Maggie in a congratulatory hug, pulling her tight, their hair practically smothering each other from the strong winds. She always thought that being a bridesmaid would be such a special experience.

"Great!" Maggie's tone turned even brighter and giddier. "Well, see, my bridesmaids are coming over to my house next week. How about I call you and let you know what day exactly and what time and all the rest of the details?"

Claire smiled. "That's just fine! I'm so excited for you, Maggie; I really am!"

Maggie grinned and nodded. "I'm so happy, Claire. I don't think I've ever been this excited about something in my entire life."

Claire kept smiling back. She really was happy for her.

Maggie moved her hand as if she was swatting away a bug, or perhaps a thought. "Anyhoo, enough about me. What are you sketching?"

It was difficult for Claire to turn her attention off such a delightful topic. "The secret garden beyond the angel oak tree, way over there," she replied, nodding and pointing toward the far, far side of the park. Giant, ancient trees shaded the area, and fog started rolling over the nearby, glistening lake. Soon, the sun would only peek above the horizon.

"Ah, it's so pretty over there!"

After they talked for several minutes, Maggie glanced at her watch and sighed. "I hate to leave when we just started talking, but I better get going. Jake said he'd be home by seven, and I haven't seen him all day. Have a delightful evening, Claire!"

"Call me if you need anything, anything at all! See you soon!" Claire replied.

"Yes, see you soon, Claire! Thank you so much!" Maggie smiled and slid off the bench, patted her skirt down, then started walking off into the sunset.

Although she was happy for Maggie, she was jealous in a way as well, even though she couldn't imagine getting married in a year and certainly didn't want to. Claire had never even had a boyfriend, and she was already sixteen. She didn't exactly want one though, either. She completely understood Maggie's worry over whether her decision was right. It was such an exhilarating yet terrifying thing. Claire and Maggie had known each other for years. They had met at that very park where Claire sat, and they immediately connected. Maggie and Claire were always searching for each other when they'd go there.

Claire had always been there for Maggie no matter what Maggie was going through. Maggie's home life wasn't exactly ideal. Perhaps that was why she was getting married so young—to get out. Maggie wasn't always there for Claire, but Claire knew her life very well, so she was understanding. Since they were older and had more responsibilities, they hadn't seen each other as often as they'd like. They had grown apart slightly, but Claire must have meant a great deal to Maggie since she asked her to be one of her bridesmaids. Maggie was always wise, so Claire knew she would make a wise decision regarding marriage.

All thoughts washed from Claire's mind when a great sketch idea came to her; she fell back into deep concentration and sketched the delicate garden for a while longer until she *knew* she was being watched. Considering it was already seven o'clock, she supposed it wouldn't be safe at the park much longer for a young lady like herself. Plus, she still needed to prepare for her brother's birthday gathering the next day. Claire cautiously took a long scan of her surroundings, then stood from the giant, willow tree-shaded bench that had never failed to please her with comfort during her times of sketching. Then she started off toward the parking lot. The park was almost dead at that time of day. Too quiet. Spooky almost. Little kids were no longer dinging their bike bells constantly, racing around, teeter-tottering from one training wheel to the other, and picnickers were no longer there feeding little bits of bread to crows. Claire never stayed that late and knew that she shouldn't have; that was when the drunks and creeps came out. Or maybe she was just paranoid. However, she was almost positive that the woman she had spotted eyeing her was still in the park. But she had only gotten a glance of her from afar, so she wasn't exactly sure. She didn't know why her body was warning her of that woman. Her mind wouldn't let her push the image of that lady out of it.

Claire walked quickly and didn't stop. She had an uneasy feeling knotting up in her stomach that warned her something wasn't right. From her terrifying gut feeling, her heart started racing like she had just finished a marathon. Panic set in, as she grew all jittery inside and started to perspire. She may have appeared as if she didn't have a single worry on her mind, but inside, Claire was scared half to death. She peered behind herself and saw a tiny, middle-aged woman walking alone. The woman's wacky workout outfit, a style Claire had never seen before, was almost humorous how mix-matched it was, and her long, brown, wild hair draped over her face, covering almost half of it. She looked away from Claire as quickly as Claire looked at her.

*That was the woman who had been eyeing her. She was sure of it.*

Claire was still on the paved path leading all the way around the park and parking lot, so she thought the lady was just getting some exercise. But it was also late for a lady to be walking by herself, Claire thought. Owls' high-pitched screeches filled the air now, and the sound of crickets chirping was becoming quite overbearing.

Quickly, Claire turned and started jogging through the large, shadowy, uneven part of the parking lot where only a handful of cars were at the late hour.

*She thought she was safe until the woman did the same.*

A strange wave of energy washed over her. She felt as though she had just run into a horror movie. *A trap*. The suspicious lady stayed back, yet Claire could tell she was following her. She just knew it and shuddered at the thought, panicking even more at the realization of it all. Adrenaline began to kick in. Claire started moving much faster, cutting through the dark bank of the lake, almost stumbling into it several times, the hidden branches smacking her in the face, causing stinging pains. Her feet kept getting caught on the roots that poked out of the ground, twisting her ankles more and more each time as she tried to lose the woman through all the brush.

*It didn't work.*

She was almost out of the parking lot, behind trees and thick brush by the main road. A streetlamp lit up the night. If only all the brush wasn't there, maybe someone may have seen her and helped. But the road wasn't even that busy, only a few cars passed by, leaving Claire in their rearview mirror.

It was dinner time, anyway. Most people were at home with their family, exactly where Claire should have been—where she longed to be.

Her sixth sense warned her that it would be a long, crazy journey until she got home. If she *ever* did, that is.

She subtly glanced behind herself one last time, and the woman was running, but not directly behind Claire anymore. Now she was on the opposite side of the brush, still in the parking lot, attempting to make Claire think nothing was wrong. She didn't realize that Claire could still see her quite clearly. Claire made a huge mistake looking back; she found herself running into someone, more specifically, a man, stocky and strong. Claire slowly peered up, meeting his deep-green, evil eyes. Her breath hitched in her chest, and she couldn't find words. Her heart pounded intensely against her chest. Before Claire could even blink, she was in his tight grasp.

*He was what that feeling deep within was warning her about.*

Leaves crunched and crumbled behind her. "Got'er, honey? Chased the poor, oblivious girl right into your arms," the woman snapped in a snarky tone.

Claire quickly whipped her head around, and her eyes widened, but all she could do was stare and try to gulp back the fear that took control of her. There stood the woman who had been chasing her, stalking her like a cat.

Finally, she snapped out of shock and regained her courage and breath. "HELP!" she screamed at the top of her lungs, thinking quickly, trying to come up with any ideas that would help her. "FIRE!" Claire screamed, hoping she would attract more attention. Her blood-curdling screams echoed in the moments of silence.

Unluckily for her, no one came to her rescue.

What was she supposed to do? She was on her own, two against one. But she had to at least try, right? If she was going to die, she would rather die trying. If she tried, maybe she'd at least wind up somewhere other than her grave.

Sharp pain shot through her arms as the man was harshly gripping her wrists. Quickly, she snapped her head over and bit him through his knit shirt, latching down hard near his shoulder. He cursed under his breath, then let go of one of her wrists, ripping his shoulder from her jaw, leaving the evidence of deep bite marks and broken skin behind. That was progress. But he started quickly dragging her, almost jogging, through the rough terrain of leaves, large sticks, and sharp pine needles, tearing her clothes and scraping her badly. *Payback*. Her adrenaline and fury only grew stronger. They were bringing her back to their car, a burgundy automobile, and it was as beat-up as an untrained boxer. No, she couldn't let that happen; that would just lead to death. Her foot gripped a giant root as the evil man stopped to make sure that the parking lot was clear, and she popped back onto her feet, ready to tango. *So those roots do come in handy sometimes!*

Now, the tiny lady gripped Claire's free wrist. She was miniature, though. She would be easier to take down, right? Claire could only hope. In one swift movement, Claire kicked the back of the woman's knees, one of her weakest spots. She fell straight to the ground with an angry grunt, her head slamming to the rough terrain, bouncing slightly, nearly taking Claire with her. But Claire was stronger than that. Claire grimaced, tensing her face. *Yikes, that had to really hurt.*

It worked on one; why not try it with the other? She did the same to the man. Claire tried to wriggle her wrist out of his grip, except she couldn't quickly enough, so she went down with him this time. He was too fast, powerful, and strong for Claire, quickly kneeling on top of her, pressing almost all of his weight onto her. She gasped for air, feeling faint, the world around her pixelating from oxygen deprivation. Then Claire saw a gun held frighteningly close to her. Had she passed out and been imagining it? Had he killed her and she was on her way to the other side? But then he got off her. She took one giant gulp of a breath. After that, everything Claire had ever taken for granted came to mind, her vision clearing. She hadn't died just yet. Then the gun came back into focus.

"You quietly come with us, or I will blow you into pieces in a split second," the muscular man whispered harshly through gritted teeth, so close she could smell his horrid breath. He had his hand on the trigger.

Claire gulped again, her heart racing faster than she had ever experienced and her chest rising and falling with each labored breath. Drowning in fear, she just lay there in complete shock, running through her thoughts. Maybe, just maybe, if she agreed to go with them, she would have a small chance of living. Or escaping. *Or killing them in the meantime.* Claire really didn't want to have to do that, though. Her heart thumped in her chest as she nodded. Heck, they might just kill her for the fun of it. She slowly got up, raising her trembling hands before her face, breathing heavily, wishing she could catch her breath. She felt like they were the cops, and she was the criminal. Warm blood leaked from her scratches and trickled down her arm, but she didn't dare move a single inch to look at them. Claire wanted to live more than anything. She loved life. She was innocent and happy. Life was great to her, and she didn't want it to end, so she walked like a dog on a lead once she heard that.

They all walked to the kidnappers' car like a happy family. If only they *really* were. Claire couldn't stand what she was doing. She couldn't stand the thought of dying either. The thought of the torture to come sent shivers down her spine. *Maybe dying would be better*. She shook her head slightly as if she could shake the thought away. *No, a stupid thought*. Claire knew that she just needed to hold on to hope. But how was that possible when she was getting kidnapped and had no clue where they would take her or what they would do with her? Tears started to pile in the corners of her eyes, reality crashing down hard on her. She slowly reached up to simply wipe her eyes, not completely thinking.

"Don't move," the evil man barked, snapping his head toward her.

Claire whimpered as tears ran down her face. She couldn't cry. Not now.

The area that they were in was empty now and pitch black.

Great for the kidnappers' sake.

Devastating for Claire.

When they got to the car, the couple commanded Claire to get into a black container so she couldn't see a thing. She hugged her legs to her chest. How long would she have to be like that? And her neck—it was so bent up and crooked. A miserable position. As she trembled, she could hear them quickly rip and stretch tape around the container to keep her inside. Then they slammed the trunk closed.

She would soon be crashing all around. If only she would have been able to see what type of car it was. At that point, would that information even help her? Claire heard the tires screech on the dry ground as the driver did a burnout while escaping the parking lot. She bounced, slid to the side of the trunk, and smashed into it. After the burnout, her whole body was twisted up, worst of all her neck. *This can't be their first time*, she thought. They were somewhat smart, though, considering they parked directly at the park entrance and left their car running. Her elbows rubbed the sides of the container, and her feet became tingly from being stuck in a single position.

Inside, it reeked of a handful of different perfumes and gas, and after some time, she could taste it.

How many of their other victims had lived? Any? And by all the scents, how many people had they targeted? The thought made her freeze. Terror got the best of her. She was scrunched up with her arms hugging her legs tightly, the only position possible, for the rest of the brutal ride. Horrible thoughts and ideas wouldn't leave her alone.

"Turn here." Claire heard the woman shout out.

"Fine," replied the man with much attitude as he took a quick, unexpected turn. Claire went flying across the trunk, hitting the opposite side. She felt a searing pain in her spine. "Ugh," she moaned.

Each time the man turned or stopped, Claire flew to the opposite side of the trunk or crashed into the back of the vehicle, causing her to cry out in pain. *Is an officer chasing us?* Claire wondered nervously. Her abductor ran over something in the road, and she practically hit the roof. She couldn't calm her racing heart or stop herself from panicking; all Claire could do was think about the terribly brutal things that could happen.

Finally, after a long, wicked, painful drive, they stopped, just as Claire thought she was going to pass out from the terribly strong gas fumes. They turned the car off, and both kidnappers quickly hopped out of the vehicle. Claire felt the car shake as they slammed the doors behind themselves.

Everything was peaceful for a short moment. Then Claire heard a motor start in the distance. Its muffled gurgle implied that it hadn't been started in a while. *A boat?* At the exact second that the thought ran through her mind, she was quickly pulled out of the car. She felt her heart as it pounded against her chest like a jack hammer. Her body trembled with fear. *Are they going to dump me in water?* She bounced as they hurriedly carried her closer and closer to the water, except they didn't dump her in. They threw her in what she assumed was a boat. Then they took off immediately. The ride felt as though the boat was gliding across the top of the water. Super smooth. *It must be a speedboat*, Claire thought.

She imagined that if she would have been on any old joy ride, the cool winds would have been whipping her hair all around. The slight mist of the water would have been refreshing.

The next thing she knew, she was being slammed around again. If they were taking her to an island, how would she even have a chance of surviving? She couldn't hear them talking very well, but what she got out of their conversation was that they had one more turn to go, and then they would be wherever they were taking her. Claire shuddered at the very thought. She certainly didn't want to be involved in any of what was happening. At the same time, she also couldn't wait to get out of the container since breathing inside was difficult. It was extremely hot inside the container, and Claire could feel her clothes sticking to her body, but she also knew that if she got out of the container it probably meant that something bad was about to happen.

*Very bad.*

Only a few seconds later, she was unexpectedly thrown off the boat by a wicked, sharp turn that knocked her into the mysterious, choppy water.

# Clove

"Roman, I don't know what's happening. I—I had this thing where I saw a girl—Claire was her name, I think. She was running through a parking lot, being chased. I just can't explain the fear that was in her eyes. The first time I saw her, she was sketching in a park. It was so peaceful. A few birds even landed on the bench she was sitting on because of her slow movements. I don't know how it escalated to this. And this girl . . . Roman, she's absolutely gorgeous. But I can tell that she doesn't think so. She had this long, reddish-brown hair that flowed perfectly over her shoulder. And her eyes, they were almost golden. Unforgettable really. Um . . . she was sitting under a huge tree; I don't recall what kind it was. It sure was giant, though," she explained to her brother. She frantically paced in front of him while picking at her nails and biting her lip.

He was pretty sure his sister said all that in one breath. "Uh, I don't know. I don't exactly have an explanation for that, Clove. A daydream maybe?"

"No, that was certainly *not* a *daydream*. It was a stinking day *nightmare*, Roman!"

Roman shook his head while shrugging his shoulders. "I don't know." He waved his hand as if waving the question away. "Don't worry about it, it's probably nothing," he finished carelessly.

Clove knew that it was something unusual because of how real it felt . . . it was as if she had been there with Claire, experiencing it all. This was something quite serious to Clove that she was trying to talk to him about, but he didn't seem too concerned as he continued to type away on his phone, smiling at it as he had been throughout their conversation. He hadn't been paying much attention at all. Roman and Clove had always been extremely close, and he was usually a good listener. This time, though, Clove thought he was texting his girlfriend, or at least that's what he called her. Clove didn't know if it was a one-sided relationship or not.

*Maybe I shouldn't even bother to worry about it*, she thought. She slipped out of his room and tried occupying herself with chores and reading her most favorite book that had caused many sleepless nights. It worked for a few hours, except later that same day, Clove started thinking about it again, and she just couldn't let it go. It was too real. A deep sense within told her that it wasn't just some daydream.

She wanted to talk to someone about it, someone who would listen. Clove didn't know anyone that she could discuss it with other than Lucas, her brother's best friend. Seriously, she couldn't think of anyone else who would help her while at the same time think she was sane; he wasn't the judgmental type. *He's almost three years older than me. Wouldn't that be weird and make me seem desperate . . . for his attention?* She debated, for what felt like an eternity, whether to discuss her peculiar situation with Lucas. Then Clove finally decided that she would just go and knock on his front door. She has always had a bit of a—a very large crush on Lucas. But he didn't know that, right? She didn't care what people would think. Clove needed help.

And besides, it was a good excuse to be around him.

"Mom?" Clove stepped out onto their back deck. The sun's rays danced across the sky, and Clove could hear the sweet chorus that the birds sang as they playfully splashed in the birdbath.

"I'm over here," Iris said quietly.

Her mother's hair was a frazzled mess with particles of just about everything in it. The old apron Clove had made for her hung from her waist, looking as though she had tried to rip it off while running outside but couldn't get it untied quickly enough. Clove slightly laughed to herself at the sight of her mother.

"Why are you whispering?" Clove blurted out, not thinking past her nose even though her mother had been in that spot a thousand times before.

"I'm trying to get a picture of this Blue Jay." Her mother didn't take her eyes off the bird for even a split second. That explained the messy hair and half-undone apron. She must have been baking or cleaning, saw the Blue Jay outside, and sprinted toward it.

"Oh." Clove wasn't surprised since her mother was always birdwatching and photographing the birds.

"Sweetie, what do you need?" Iris asked.

"I was just coming to tell you I'm going to Lucas's house for a few minutes." She bit her lip, swaying her hips with her hands intertwined behind her, hoping her mother wouldn't ask why.

"Okay?" Iris looked confused but didn't question her.

It wasn't horribly strange, even though Clove and Lucas rarely ever hung out. They didn't mind each other, but their age gap made the friendship a bit weird. Her mother liked Lucas. She knew he was a good kid. Clove never really went to his house, only once in a blue moon. Sometimes she would hang out with him and her brother but that wasn't very often either. Lucas lived only a few houses down the street. He and Roman had been friends since, well, forever.

Clove quickly ran inside, slipped on her worn-out, patchwork Vans, and then she was out the door. As Clove walked down her driveway, she felt the heat from the sun on her shoulders, warming her body. The mild breeze blew her hair away from her face. She heard her dog begin to bark from inside as she walked down the sidewalk.

Clove was excited to see Lucas. She hadn't seen him in quite a while. It took about half a second to get to his house since he lived so close. Clove had always dreamed of having a boyfriend on the same street as her, but her wish seemed out of reach. Then she started falling really hard for Lucas the past year and hoped that one day he would be that guy.

Ugh, but the stupid age gap . . . and Lucas being *way* out of her league.

She stared nervously at his family's aged, brick house and the delicate purple and yellow flowers growing beneath their windows that swayed in the wind. As she got farther and farther up the driveway, she heard their fountain quickly trickling down its textured front and splashing back into itself. However, Clove had failed to notice that their large SUV wasn't in the driveway until she got to the porch. She panicked, freezing for a second. At that moment, she should have turned away and waited until later. Clove still decided to go up to the door because she assumed Lucas and his mom were most likely home and his father had the vehicle. The wind was picking up, and the old rocking chairs on his large porch creaked and gave Clove quite the jump scare.

What if they had already seen her lurking around? *It would be strange for me to turn back now*, she thought. She was putting herself under pressure. Once Clove reached the front door, she knocked, and the door cracked open after a while. In that time of waiting, she wondered if she should duck and run, but that would be like a ding-dong ditch if anyone was home. What a jerk that would make her. *A little chicken.*

"Oh, it's you," Lucas said. He quickly closed the door so that he was able to unlock the chain lock. How very . . . welcoming. Then he reopened it—his shirtless, defined, muscular build distracting Clove for a long moment. His hair was messy, sticking every which way, like he had showered, dried it, and hadn't brushed it. Clove figured it was because he had just been lying around.

"Who else would it be?" She laughed. Her eyes lingered over his body before meeting his eyes. She felt stupid after thinking about how many other people it could have been at his door. "Are you busy? Are your—your parents home?" Clove had to know. She held her hands behind her back, sinking her nails deep into her palms, leaving indentations.

"No, but uh . . . come on in, I don't think they'll mind," he said through a yawn. He spun around, motioning for Clove to follow him in.

"Did I wake you?" She was attempting to make conversation in the moment of awkwardness.

"Nope, I was just watching a movie," he said. He turned back toward Clove. "Half falling asleep!" he mumbled as he smirked.

"Oh, I'm—I'm sorry."

"Oh no, don't be."

Clove wondered if it was such a good idea to be in a house alone with him. Really, she knew the answer. But it was Lucas; she felt safe around him. *He would never ever hurt me, right? I've known him for years*, she thought.

"Would you like to sit here or hang out in my room?" he questioned.

Clove quickly peered around the sitting room that was very close to them. His mother was a plant addict. Plants hung from almost every vacant spot in the room. Some of them even wrapped perfectly around the curtain rods. A few very colorful succulents were placed on the low windowsill, soaking up the sunlight. As Clove looked over toward their coffee table, his cute, tiny, tabby cat poked its head out from under the table, where it lay in its hammock. Clove could only wish to have their gorgeous, packed bookcase that reached the ceiling.

"Your choice."

Lucas shrugged his shoulders after a moment of thought. "Eh, let's go in my room."

*His room?* Clove thought, knowing that she couldn't exactly turn back now. "Okay," her voice squeaked. As they headed up to Lucas's room, the living room curtains made a loud, frightening, whooshing sound as they floated in the breeze, which made Clove jump. She glanced back, not recalling the open windows or a fan being on when she was just in there. However, both were. Looking back, she noticed a few framed photos of Lucas that she hadn't seen a few moments earlier, that she practically couldn't take her eyes off. She never got tired of seeing his gorgeous, ocean-blue eyes or bleach-blonde hair, which was almost the color of sugar sand but much softer. Not that she had felt it, no; she just imagined it was soft.

Clove started to feel clammy. "Is it hot in here?" She tried to play it cool.

He looked at her while walking up the stairs, then touched her shoulder. "God, you are really warm. Are you feeling alright?"

"Yes, other than feeling like I am in a fire." Clove giggled nervously.

He stopped dead in his tracks, catching on to the reason behind what was happening, but he brushed it off and kept his distance. Lucas would *never* want to make her nervous or uncomfortable. And he would *never, ever* hurt her.

Lucas quickly turned his tower-fan toward Clove when they entered his room, hoping it would help Clove cool down. Then he jumped onto his bed and motioned for Clove to grab his desk chair.

"Thanks for that." Clove pointed to the fan, then looked throughout Lucas's large room, glancing from the baseball trophies that sat on a floating shelf above his bed to the wall art of famous athletes and inspirational quotes that she hadn't remembered being there before, then back to Lucas, who lay on his all black bed with its one and only colorful pillow.

"No problem," he said lazily. "So, what's so important that you came to *me*?" He half-laughed.

"Well . . ." She took a long, deep breath, then started explaining, deep in detail.

"Hm." He raised an eyebrow when she paused momentarily, just as confused as her.

*Please don't let him think I am a psycho.*

"Where were you when this happened?" He was very curious.

"Both times I was by our local park."

"How long ago?"

"Maybe . . . a week or two ago."

"Does the park from the . . . whatever it was . . . look the same as our local one?" Lucas asked.

"Similar. Not the exact same, but quite similar," she finally said after thinking. Then she began to ponder on the situation even more. It was all so strange.

*Why me?*

"Clove, you know, I had this friend years ago who said she was reincarnated, or *she* wasn't reincarnated; someone was reincarnated into her. It sounds similar to what's happening to you. Just an idea." Lucas shrugged his shoulders.

Clove narrowed her eyes at him. "What exactly does that mean?" She scanned Lucas's room again, her eyes landing on a picture of his girlfriend. She was drop-dead gorgeous. Her pencil-straight, black hair reached down to her hips, her perfectly arched eyebrows framed her face beautifully, and her satin-like skin was as clear as a cloudless sky. And her sea-green eyes—they definitely looked like they held one heck of a secret. That was for sure. But what *exactly* was that secret?

"Basically, it's being rebirthed into a different body. I don't know exactly what it is; you should search it up."

"Huh, okay. Interesting."

"I've read a bit about it, and it does sound very similar to what you're experiencing. But it could also be thousands of other things, you know?" Lucas sort of laughed.

"Yeah, I know." Out of nowhere, Clove's hazel eyes glazed over. She blinked rapidly several times, but she was going to zone out no matter what. "What's wrong?" She heard Lucas ask, but it was muffled, as if she had cotton balls stuffed in her ears. She could feel how much Lucas ached for her from the tone of his voice—full of pure sympathy. *It was happening again.* This time, it was even worse. She saw Claire unexpectedly run into the arms of a tall, muscular man. Clove could hear Claire's high-pitched screams for help and watched as the man threatened to kill Claire, causing her to do as he said. Clove clenched her teeth as she saw the woman who had been chasing Claire now running up behind her.

The man and woman were working on the evil plan together. *Accomplices.*

Within the blink of an eye, the daydream, the flashback, the vision—or whatever it was, was over. Clove gave Lucas a worried stare and Lucas gave it right back to her.

"Let me guess, another one?" he asked.

She nodded slowly, explaining exactly what she saw.

"I wonder why the first two times these things happened you were by the park, and now it randomly just happened while you're sitting here."

"Hm," Clove mumbled. "I didn't think about that. I don't know. That is kinda strange," she remarked, glancing down at her watch. "Well, thanks for the information, but I've got to get go—"

"Hey, uh . . ." Lucas's voice was shaky. "Don't tell your brother that you came over and that my parents weren't home, okay?"

"Okay? W—why is that?"

"Uh, just don't tell him, pretty please!" He gave her a toothy smile.

Clove could hear the nervousness in his voice, as if her brother would do something to Lucas if he knew the two of them hung out alone. "Okay, well, I need to head home. Thank you for listening."

Clove was a bit stumped as to why he didn't want Roman to know that they hung out alone. Sure, there were a couple obvious reasons—Roman being protective of her . . . Lucas being older than her. But would it truly bother Roman that much?

As she approached her house, so many thoughts were rushing through her mind that she hadn't even noticed her brother sitting on their front porch talking to his so-called girlfriend on the phone.

"What am I, invisible?" he mumbled.

She gasped, throwing a hand to her heart, stumbling backward. "Goodness, you scared me, Roman!"

"You ignored me!" he snapped. He threw one of his hands up in the air.

"Sorry, I didn't see you!" Clove stepped inside.

"It's fine, whatever." He sort of brushed it off.

*Thank God he didn't ask about me being away,* she thought, finally letting go of a stressed breath.

As she stepped into the house, her mother caught her slightly off guard. "Clove?" asked her mother.

The girl couldn't catch a break.

The aroma of garlic and fresh herbs scented the air. Her mom must have been in the kitchen cooking dinner.

"Uh-huh?" Clove answered.

"Please set the table. Lucas and his parents are coming over for dinner!" her mother remarked, smiling, not knowing the panic that Clove was going through.

Clove's breath hitched in her chest. She wanted to laugh but not for a happy reason. "Uh, did you say Lucas?" Just as much as she did want it to be him, she also didn't.

"Mhmm. Indeed, I did."

*Crap.*

"Why, is there a problem with that?" Iris's tone was serious.

"No, no," Clove's voice cracked. "Not at all. I just hadn't heard anything about this before now, that's all."

"Oh, well, we haven't had them over in a while, so I figured it would be nice to invite them over tonight. It was a spur-of-the-moment kind of thing! I just asked Candy a few minutes ago."

That's why Lucas hadn't said anything to Clove about it.

"Ah, I see. How nice! Now, what time are they coming over?"

"About six. Get ready!"

"I will, right when I'm done!" She managed a fake smile. Hundreds of worries were rushing through her brain. There was no way that Roman would not find out about the earlier situation; Clove just knew it. But she would try to have a decent night and not stress . . . too much, at least. Once she finished her chores downstairs, she quickly changed into a summery, floral dress. Then she wrapped her strawberry-blonde hair into a bun and pulled out her framing hairs. She knew it was hopeless, but she would at least try!

Just as Clove walked out of her bedroom, the doorbell rang. "I'll get it!" she called out. She practically flew down the stairs. She wrapped her hand around the cold door handle and ripped it open.

*Talk about desperate.* She even got to the door before their dog.

"You look delightful, darling!" Lucas's mother, Candy, said. Large, yet dainty gold hoops hung from Candy's ears. Her bright pink lipstick added a nice pop of color to her look.

A soft smile set on Clove's face. "Thank you!"

Instead of Clove turning her attention to Lucas's mother or father, she admired Lucas. Him and his dreaminess. Sleek black clothing hugged his body in all the right ways. She watched the way his sculpted cheeks moved as he smiled—how he clenched his teeth, tightening his jawline when he saw Roman.

*Ugh, his lips are so perfect.*

Lucas looked her up and down, trapping her in his eyes, his ocean-blue eyes, then moved to stand next to her. He caught Clove off guard, pulling every last breath from her lungs. She prayed that he hadn't seen her practically drooling over him.

After she was able to pull herself together and collect her words, Clove subtly whispered, "What are we going to do? It's going to come up at dinner. I just know that it will."

"Yeah, just . . ." He ran his hand through his now slicked-back hair. "Just tell them I didn't answer the door and you were hanging out in your garden," he finally said.

"Alright," Clove responded in a very calm, unsure tone, not loving that she was going to lie.

Roman passed them again, giving Clove a weird look, then walked away. He was in the middle of getting himself ready for dinner.

"Uh . . . I'll go hang out with him so that he doesn't start getting curious." Lucas pointed toward the back of the house, then spun on his heels and walked away as Clove smiled and nodded.

Clove so badly wanted to tag along behind Lucas and go hang out with him and her brother, but at the same time, she knew for a fact that it was a bad idea. So instead, she went and hung out with the parents.

Candy's crazy-tight ponytail swung back and forth as she turned her head to look at Clove as Clove entered the kitchen. "Oh, you are just so beautiful!" Candy said.

Clove gave her a polite, blushing smile. *Am I really?* Clove wondered.

"How come you aren't hanging out with the boys?" Iris asked.

Clove just shook her head and shrugged the question off, hoping her mother wouldn't question her further. She went over to the dinner table and slipped into the cool seat, waiting for their dinner to finish.

Iris tensed her jaw and shrugged like Clove while looking at Candy. Sometimes she simply couldn't explain her children's actions.

Clove quietly watched the parents converse. It was funny because Candy looked almost old enough to be Iris's mother. She'd had Lucas later in life, so late that she didn't think she had a chance at getting pregnant, but after so many years of longing to be a mother, she finally got her sweet boy. But she didn't look old in the crow's feet near her eyes and sagging skin under her chin way. Instead, her grey hairs near her scalp paired with her cat-eye glasses and bold lipstick said "I'm going to look sophisticated and classy while I age." Clove admired Candy's classy aura.

The sudden buzz of the oven timer put an instant stop to what seemed to be the adults' never-ending chatter. Candy raised her eyebrow at Iris to see if the meal was ready. Iris gave her a slow nod and smiled.

Candy hurried over to the staircase. "Roman, Lucas, dinner!"

The quick rush of feet pounding against the stairs blocked out the sound of chatter and laughter for a moment. They all gathered plenty of food onto their plates and eventually seated themselves accordingly. But as Lucas strolled over to the table, he balanced his plate on three fingers and then practically tossed it to his other hand because it was so hot. Clove laughed and shook her head.

Unfortunately, what they wished wouldn't happen, happened; the earlier situation came up at dinner. "Oh yeah, Clove, didn't you go over to see Lucas today?" her mother eventually asked.

Lucas looked up from his plate of steaming lasagna with a blank expression covering his face, gulping back the slight bit of fear that was sprouting within him. He glanced toward Clove, catching her eye. She could clearly tell he was on edge.

Clove raised an eyebrow. "I did, but no one answered," she said slowly, trying her best to sound convincing.

Lucas interrupted the conversation, "She must have come over when I was watching a movie. I had it on really loud."

"Then why were you down there so long?" Roman questioned Clove like he was interrogating a criminal, ignoring Lucas's statement.

"I wasn't. When you saw me, I was coming from our garden."

"Okay, whatever," Roman mumbled, raising an eyebrow at Clove and Lucas. Obviously unconvinced, he looked back down toward his plate, studying what he would eat next.

Luckily, Candy changed the subject at the perfect moment before things got a little heated. After that, the rest of the dinner was peaceful and even fun.

The Lynches and the Rileys hadn't had one of those dinners together in a very long time. Too long. Whenever they all had dinner together, it always reminded Clove of the very first time they all officially met. It was years ago, their first barbecue with Lucas's family. Iris invited them over to get to know them. She was like that, friendly with everyone. When the night of the get together came, and the doorbell rang, Clove rushed down the stairs, not knowing she was about to collide with her dream boy. In a sort of shy way, she cracked the door open. When she was met with Candy's kind face, she knew it was safe to open it all the way. Then she adjusted her gaze to the little person just like her who stood silently next to Candy. She swallowed. It was like the breath in her lungs just . . . disappeared. That always happened when she saw Lucas, even if it was only for a moment of time. She didn't know what to say or do. Thank God her mother trailed closely behind her, swooping Clove up into her arms. Her mother kissed her on the cheek. "Clove, Lucas. Lucas, Clove," her mother introduced them. "The boys will get along so well, I'm sure of it!" Iris smiled happily. The whole time, Clove was pretty sure she hadn't stopped looking at Lucas. She wasn't even sure if she had blinked. He smiled so genuinely at her, and she was almost jealous of how long and luscious his eyelashes were. He was just so . . . cute. And ever since, she hasn't been able to get Lucas off her mind.

After dinner, after everyone left, Clove was sitting on her bed, doing some research on reincarnation, when Roman barged in.

"Don't lie to me, Clove. What's going on?" he demanded.

She snapped her head up at him, searching his eyes, looking puzzled.

"Don't even play stupid." He let his head fall back, annoyed, almost laughing. "You know what I'm talking about. You know you went to his house earlier, and he answered the door. You weren't *just in our backyard*," Roman said, forming hand quotations. He was *ticked.*

"Yes, I certainly did go to his house earlier, but no one answered. Seriously Roman, quit! Why do you even care so much?"

Roman sat on her bed and leaned so close to her that she could almost smell his breath. "You're off limits to him, forever. I don't trust him enough. And if he were to ever hurt you, just know, there's not much I'm afraid to do to protect you," he stated in the most serious tone she had ever heard from him.

Geez, why was he going off on her like that? She never thought that he would get that ticked. *What had Lucas done?*

"Roman, I'm thirteen. Heck, basically fourteen. Two more months. And . . . it's *Lucas* that we are talking about! I'm sorry, but you are completely overreacting."

"I'm not overreacting!" He slammed his fist on her bedside table. "You need to learn these things. Stuff happens, you know."

"I know!" Clove shouted back.

"Understand?"

"Yes." Really, she only said yes to shut him up. He was not her parent, so she certainly didn't have to listen to him.

"Good night." Roman started to leave her bedroom.

Clove was relieved he was leaving. "Good nigh—"

Roman interrupted Clove, "Okay, maybe he wouldn't be completely off limits when you're older. You're too young now, though."

Clove gave him a very strange glare. *Why such a quick change of heart?* She wondered. *Weirdo.*

"I don't really care, but thanks for the heads up; I really appreciate it!" Clove rolled her eyes, trying to act as if she had no interest in Lucas.

Then Roman finally left her room, closing the door almost all the way.

*Yes!*

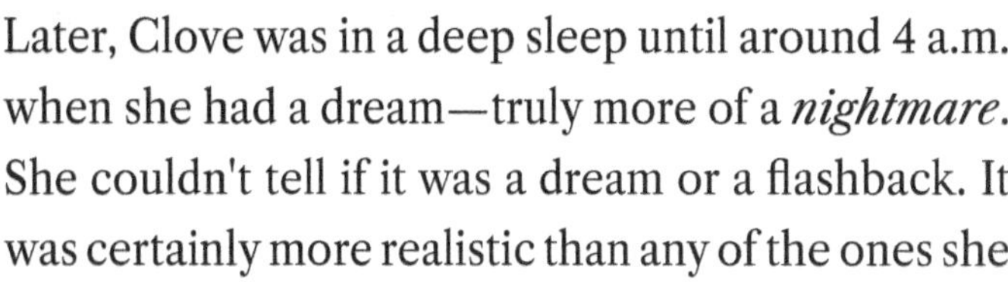

Later, Clove was in a deep sleep until around 4 a.m. when she had a dream—truly more of a *nightmare*. She couldn't tell if it was a dream or a flashback. It was certainly more realistic than any of the ones she had before. She watched helplessly as Claire was threatened into getting into a container in the trunk of her kidnapper's beat-up, rust-covered Plymouth Special Deluxe. Sadly, there was not a single person in sight to help. The car was grimy; the dented bumper was held on by some sort of strap. Clove swore that she could smell perfumes, just slightly, like scents that were carried through the atmosphere with a summer breeze. It was freaky. They had done this before, Clove thought, and so did Claire. They were prepared.

As quickly as the drop of a pencil, they were out of the parking lot. From such rapid speeds, Claire would slam into the opposite side of the trunk every turn, and every speed bump was brutal. The ride was petrifying. They even cut through the woods at one point, running over a dead raccoon, as the trees scraped the side of their car, causing a very high-pitched screech. Clove shuddered at the thought of how bruised poor Claire would be after all the crashing around in the car.

Clove could see that the trunk was loosely held shut by a bungee cord that looked like it would pop off at any second. She didn't want Claire to bounce out of the car if the trunk popped open, but at the same time, she did. It would be rough when Claire hit the ground, falling from such a quickly moving vehicle, but it could possibly save her life in the long run.

She couldn't imagine Claire's fear. Clove wasn't even there, and her heart was about to pound out of her chest.

After what felt like hours, they finally came to a rough stop at a dock. The sky was absent of any stars. It was the sort of dark where you couldn't see if a person was standing a foot in front of you. It was a rural area—no streetlights or high beams from cars passing by because there were none. The noise of an old dock wobbling back and forth in the lake's dark waters masked the peaceful sounds of trees swaying in the warm nighttime breeze, frogs croaking, and small creatures rustling leaves around.

Since the area was like one big abyss, Clove really couldn't see much at all around the boat. Large clouds filled the sky, blocking the moon from reflecting off the lake. The fog was thick, and the atmosphere was simply dark. Gloomy. *Chilling*. But the one thing that she could see was that they were parked on a slight hill, far off the road, far enough out that no one would hear Claire's cries.

Both of Claire's abductors jumped out of the car. The woman put gas in the dingy speedboat, and the man tried to start it. He seemed slightly confused, like it wasn't familiar to him. *Is it even theirs? Or are they going to steal it?* After a few tries, it started running loudly; the type of loudness that rumbles the ground and creeps up into your body.

Their hands trembling and sweaty, they carried the container over to the boat, almost dropping Claire twice and then almost stumbling off the dock. No matter how often they did it, they never knew if that was the night they would be *caught. Arrested. Captured* for their *dark, sinister* crimes.

Clove watched closely as they threw Claire into the boat and sped away. The same way they had left the parking lot: break-neck fast and dangerous. The man made several sharp turns. One time, Clove knew the move must have hurt Claire. Clove could see the container that held Claire and knew there wasn't a way for Claire to escape.

Clove didn't want to watch it anymore. Still, she felt an odd longing pulling her deeper and deeper into it, a sort of strange connection that made her unable to wake up or pull away from the terrible nightmare of a scene. Therefore, she had *no* choice.

It was the most excruciating boat ride Claire had ever been on, and it was the most excruciating thing that Clove had ever watched. Claire wished she had never gone to the park that night. When Claire flew off the boat into the deep, dark waters of the open ocean, Clove practically lost her breath along with Claire as she hit the chilly water, entering with a loud thunk and splash.

Clove finally woke up from *whatever the heck that was*, clutching her chest as it rose and fell with each labored breath she took. It made her feel as though she could relate to Claire. If she was little, she would have run to her parents' room, crying from the dreadful nightmare. Now, she wasn't afraid, exactly; she just wanted answers and peace.

*Why, why her? Were these things a sign of something?*

*Or was she just going crazy?*

# Claire

Claire knew she was close to death, but she still had a small amount of hope left in her delicate, exhausted, trembling body. The container was almost halfway filled with water, and she was completely panicked, gasping for air as water gushed in with each wave—the waves that the boat's wake caused. She had punched the container several times, and it wouldn't budge. It was only letting more and more water in. But she put the last of her strength into her fists, and finally, it cracked. She sighed in relief. Claire pushed, and punched, and kicked at the top as hard as possible. Finally, finally, she made a big enough opening to get out.

Claire was so happy she wanted to cry.

She had sunk deep. Claire wasn't a fan of the water at all. It was too dark and mysterious for her; she especially didn't like water when she couldn't see to the bottom. And she definitely couldn't where she was. She tried to swim her weak body to the top, knowing she wasn't very good at treading water. After what felt like an eternity of struggling, she was there, gasping for air as she popped her head out of the water, the cool breeze smacking her in the face.

While treading the water that surrounded her the best she could, sinking really, not knowing what was beneath her or where she was, she could see the speedboat's blinding lights ahead.

*Think, Claire, think.*

Before she knew it, the speedboat's light was adjusted and shone right on her.

She squinted against it, but it was crazy bright. With only seconds to spare and little clue on what to do, she took a long, deep breath and dove into the cloudy water. Claire hadn't even caught her breath yet from the first time she went under. And now again? Her hope was draining quickly. They had most likely already seen her. Could she ever get a break to breathe for just a minute?

As Claire saw the boat's light getting closer, she felt something latch on tightly to her leg. Immediately, her heart began to beat stronger, and she began to kick her leg frantically, trying to get whatever it was that had a hold of her to release its grip. Funny enough, it felt like the grip of warm hands. As the moments went by, she subconsciously kicked her leg less and less—her heartbeat returned to a normal pace. While Claire was nervous, she also felt at ease, not threatened or in danger, just at ease. In all the chaos she felt a safe presence wash over her. It was the oddest thing. And her leg didn't hurt, so she didn't worry that it was a shark. It was some sort of sea creature, she assumed. She just couldn't see what it was because of how dark and cloudy the water appeared. There was a voice deep within Claire that told her she was going to be okay and that her situation was about to improve. *She just had to hold tight.* She sure didn't believe the voice, though.

The boat was quickly getting closer and closer. Claire was running out of oxygen fast and becoming light-headed. The grip on her leg had loosened, but then suddenly it yanked her leg one more powerfully, hard time. Before she knew it, before she could think twice about drowning or dying, she was being pulled through some sort of tube at the speed of sound.

Her heart sank, and she thought that perhaps her stomach was in her throat. Crazy flashing lights made her eyes go haywire. She felt like she was going to faint and throw up at the same time. But it stopped as quickly as it started.

She slammed into a wall, coming to a quick halt. Disoriented. Weak. Exhausted. Claire was shocked that she hadn't drowned in the water in the tube.

*How had the water not been forced up her nose?* That was practically impossible. She hadn't even been exhaling.

"Ugh, ow, my leg," Claire moaned. She cradled her leg, not knowing how she could even feel it after it had gone numb from being bent for so long. And the strangest thing happened; her scratches were almost healed. She traced her finger along the sides of the scratches on her shin. They felt weird, but they weren't sore anymore. *Scars.* Her leg though, well, that was the least of her worries after she looked up.

"You're extremely lucky I found you early enough. You were close to being taken to your death," said a tall, still, shadowy figure floating in front of Claire.

Claire gasped and turned as gray as a gloomy sky. "Who—what—if you're what—what I think you are . . . I've got to be dreaming," Claire was finally able to say. She almost laughed.

"A mermaid?" the woman asked with a raised eyebrow and tilted head.

Trembling, Claire nodded slowly.

"One hundred percent," the mysterious being said.

She had to be going crazy. *This must be a joke or death*, she thought. Claire's thoughts were definitely wandering. The thought of death, especially, petrified her.

Trying to collect her thoughts, Claire eagerly scanned the strange area she was in. The dimness, however, challenged her vision. The atmosphere gave an odd illusion that a cloud was floating above. She could only see the woman's silhouette. Then she tried to float through the cloudy wall that was in front of her.

"Child, what are you trying to do?" The mermaid quietly chuckled. She shook her head, while bringing up her thin, delicate hand to cover her mouth.

"Trying to see if I'm dreaming or if I died." Claire was panicking at the thought of death.

"You are not at all dreaming or dead, just extremely fortunate." She smiled.

"But—but how? I—I never thought that your kind was truly real." Claire wanted to run, hide—get to safety—disappear into thin air.

"Well, you see, I'm floating right here. If that's not enough proof for you, I don't know what is!" The mermaid slightly chuckled again.

Claire raised her hand in defense. "No, no! There's no way this is real. How am I breathing underwater?" Claire asked with wide eyes.

"A spell. Any other questions?"

*But if I'm dreaming, I would also be able to breathe underwater, right?* The thought crossed her mind for a moment.

"Um . . . your name?" Claire answered, gazing at her in shock.

"My name is Coralia. Nice to meet you, Claire."

Claire shook the mermaid's hand as her eyes grew larger. "I—I didn't tell you my name," she remarked, even more confused than she had been.

The woman gestured to Claire's necklace.

"Oh!" Claire sighed in relief, yet her heart was still fluttery, her mind still scrambled, and her body still trembling slightly. She had never felt so out of control of her own body.

"Follow me."

"Wait, I can't. I need to get home—" Claire pointed toward the wall behind her as if there was a door there. Had she come through that wall? Or was that simply just where she landed? "My parents probably already reported me missing. I'm sure of it. And I—I need to go."

"Claire, it's not exactly safe out there. They'll capture you again if you go back through that portal. At least stay until morning."

Claire had completely forgotten that her kidnappers were on the lookout for her.

"How do you know that I was kidnapped?" Claire was so confused as to what was happening.

"Rescuing people who have been kidnapped is one of my jobs, dear." Cora smiled, looking as though she was thinking back to all the people she had saved.

Claire didn't know what to say or what to do. She just nodded. She had the funniest and strongest gut feeling she had ever experienced in her entire life. Claire felt she could trust the mermaid, like her soul wouldn't let her go any other way—as if there was a heavy rope around her torso being yanked. She could physically feel it. Sense it.

"Are you hungry?"

"A bit, yes," Claire stated with a slight nod, very hesitant on whether to take food from her—trust her.

*Follow Coralia. She is your only hope.*

"Well then, in that case, why don't I bring you to my home?"

"Where *are* we exactly?" Claire wondered, scanning the area, curious as ever and frightened. When she looked up, she could tell they were in a giant dome. It was dark out, just like the human world, but a bit of light shone through to meet her eyes. *No way that's the moon.* It appeared frosted in certain areas on the top and sides of the dome, blocking Claire from a completely clear view of the outside. *It isn't actually ice, right? That isn't possible.*

"Oh, this place has many purposes, Claire," Coralia answered with a soft smile. She was quite short and straightforward when she spoke, but in a way, she had a nurturing aura.

As they swam, Claire took a long look around the dome. On the inside, odd, richly-colored plants draped down from the ceiling, slowly swaying back and forth. It was almost mesmerizing. *Peaceful.* It reminded Claire of fancy flowers hanging from a ballroom ceiling. As they continued swimming through the dome, yellow corals rose up and then fell back into the sugar sand on the sides of the hall as they passed, as if they had a sensor. But by the time Claire looked back, they were gone. She shook the confusion off, figuring they were designed by magic or a spell, or she was just going crazy. Oh, how she longed for it all to be real.

Then Claire turned her head quickly around a corner to sneak a peek into one of the rooms, but the hollow-like walls and tiny window on the ship-like door to the room were almost frosted over, just like the ceiling. But it didn't look like ice. It looked as though clouds had fallen from the sky and had been sucked into the hollowness of the clear walls to create privacy for certain rooms.

*Is someone in there? Are they okay?* Claire shuddered at the thought.

Claire could only slightly see outside of the dome through the flowers descending from the ceiling and the cloudy patches all around. She was dying to get out of there. Oh, how she prayed that it was all she thought it would be and people weren't waiting just outside the door to harm her.

After a while, Cora glanced back toward Claire, who couldn't swim as quickly and gracefully as her. "After you eat, I'll show you to your guest room."

Claire was beginning to feel as if she was swimming through mud, her arms feeling heavy. "Uh . . ." It took Claire a moment to gather her words. "Thank you . . . so much. You have no clue how much I appreciate it. You—you saved my life."

*Claire hoped that those words were true.* "Is it safe for me down here?"

"To an extent . . ." Cora paused. "Certainly safer than it is up there at any time." She pointed upward, toward the human world. "Just remember not to touch any corals," she added.

Claire gave her a funny look. To Claire, the plants hanging from the ceiling did not at all look like what corals were described to be.

Cora pointed toward the ones that were coming up beside them in waves. "They can dissolve you quickly."

"Oh my, you're just joking, right?"

"No."

*Oh boy.*

Claire was starting to really wonder if she would make it out alive.

*You're just dreaming . . . or dead.*

Wouldn't bits and pieces of the corals on the ceiling fall and float down to her? That would count as touching them. Claire sighed and shook her head. *No, Cora wouldn't have saved me just for me to be dissolved by corals . . . right?*

The swim to the exit of the dome was quite peaceful. Claire's eyes widened when they passed a few mermaids and mermen who waved. Their beautiful, bronze skin shimmered as they moved, and the exquisite gemstones embedded in their tails sparkled like stars in the evening sky. Claire hardly blinked at all as she stared at them as they swam by. She didn't want to be rude, but there were merfolk three feet from her. *Who* wouldn't stare? They *seem* friendly, she thought. Why were they so accepting of her? It was as if it was *normal* for her to be down there.

Everything was almost perfect. *Too perfect.*

Claire tried her best to keep her head straight and not look around too much because she wasn't sure how much she was and wasn't supposed to see, and the last thing she wanted to find out was the consequence of seeing something forbidden to her eyes. Most of the walls were filled with the mysterious white substance; therefore, Claire didn't have a clear view of what was locked away in the rooms.

After some time, Claire's gaze fell to her legs. The scratches were practically healed! She had forgotten about them for a while. "Um, Coralia?"

Cora swiftly whipped around in the water, meeting Claire's eyes. The thousands of little bubbles she made rose to the top of the giant dome. "Yes?" She tilted her head and craned her neck out toward Claire.

Claire almost ran into Cora because of how quickly Cora stopped and whipped around. "You see, I had some quite deep scratches on my legs and some on my arms. Did—did—what happened?"

Coralia narrowed her eyes and looked at the bruises and scrapes and scars. "Well, whenever someone is brought through one of our portals, they are healed while they are in it."

Claire slowly nodded, and Cora turned back around.

*Wow*. So *that* was a portal. *Interesting*.

It was a bit hard for Claire to keep up with Coralia since she wasn't used to swimming very much. As Claire was about to ask if they could take a break, they finally got to the stained-glass doors that led to the outside of the merfolk world. The doors were round and placed several feet up from the ground. Claire thought that perhaps they were partly made from sea glass.

*Finally*.

"Welcome to the rest of our world, Claire!" A proud smile spread across Coralia's features.

Once they got outside, Claire was taken aback by the drastic temperature change, a shock to the heart. Like jumping from a hot tub into a cool pool, freezing her to the bone for a moment. Claire shivered as she floated in place for a very long time, taking it all in, fascinated, to say the least. The snow-white sand was spread out ever so evenly across the immaculate seabed. Claire imagined reaching down and touching the sand—she thought it would feel soft, even powdery, perhaps.

She turned around to face the building they had just exited. It looked just like clouds all over the dome. *What is it exactly? Is it always like that?* Claire wanted to ask, but at the same time, she didn't. And Cora didn't exactly seem like she wanted to throw the information out to Claire either.

Claire had a sense of smell there; it was really the strangest thing. It concerned her too. She thought that it was odd that the world didn't carry a fishy smell along with it. Instead, it carried the earthy scent that often accompanied rainfall. She adored that smell while sitting on her giant porch in her hammock, watching the rain come down. It was so magical to her. It took her to a different place. She would go back there, *right?*

She couldn't dwell on that now.

As she whipped back around in the water, a fish nearly smacked her. That would have hurt. She chuckled, realizing that her jaw was still ajar in amazement. The fish didn't seem to be afraid of the merfolk or her at all.

Corals spread across the seabed, and seaweed was swaying high and low. To Claire, it was not at all how the deep sea was explained to be. Even through the darkness, she could see how crystal clear the water was. Several schools of what Cora said were parrotfish, and a dolphin, swam past peacefully as they were heading to Coralia's house. Claire had never been that close to a dolphin in her life. She always thought that they were such special creatures.

Claire searched the area constantly, but because of the time of night it was, she could only see the outline of what looked like caves, sea plants, ginormous boulders, and the distant glowing homes ahead.

"See, we only let certain creatures into our world," Cora informed.

"That's why I don't see many common fish."

"Correct." Coralia pointed ahead. They were getting close to her house now.

*That's her house? A bottle in which you would send a message across the sea? But how did it get* **so** *big?* Its exaggerated size made Claire think that once again she was in a dream.

Claire spotted movement inside the bottle but was clueless as to what it was. Then they got even closer. Blobs of something unknown were glowing on Cora's home. As they approached the porthole-like front door, Claire was able to examine the blobs at a closer view, realizing that they were different-sized octopi, ones that illuminated and lit up the night. She watched them slowly moving around, getting situated. Claire imagined that if it was her home, she wouldn't be able to ever fall asleep, for watching the glowing creatures was so magically unreal. However, while she could watch them for a lifetime, she was so eager to get inside too. Her eyelids were growing heavy—her stomach grumbly and her mind boggled. Claire looked about, enjoying the tranquility of the evening, as it took Cora a moment to unlatch the gold lock on the door. Specks of light were dotted around here and there and out in the distance. *More glowing sea life?*

Claire heard a quiet squeak as Coralia opened the door. A fishy smell flooded her nostrils. "Lou, we have a guest," Coralia hollered as they entered the house.

A large merman floated out of one of the rooms separated by archways. His raven-black hair instantly reminded Claire of her little brother—in turn, reminding her that she was probably going to miss his birthday party. She tuned out everything around her for a moment, a wave of sadness washing over her. *No.* She had to remember the positive. Claire peered back up at Lou, forcing a smile.

Lou's gray eyes sparkled like a brilliant gemstone. Unlike Cora's violet tail, his was deep green fading into navy blue, which somehow perfectly complimented his strong features and onyx hair. His eyebrows rose as his eyes widened when he saw Claire. "Why, hello!" he remarked with a slight smile pulling at the corners of his mouth. He then stuck his hand out to greet her. "Good to meet you; I'm Lou."

They hooked thumbs when they shook hands. *Interesting. Weird.*

Claire nodded. "Nice to meet you as well. I'm Cla—"

"Claire?" Lou asked.

"You saw the necklace?" She wasn't so alarmed that time.

"Indeed, I did," he answered with a chuckle and nod.

Then Cora glanced at him. "Claire is going to have dinner with us."

"Ah, well tonight I made stuffed shells along with seaweed salad!" he exclaimed very proudly.

Claire raised an eyebrow as an unsettling expression crossed her face.

"Don't worry; it's not bad." Coralia smiled softly.

"Not to you," Claire mumbled under her breath while smiling like she didn't have a single worry.

She took a breath in, taking in all the peculiar scents of their dinner.

Thankfully, neither Coralia nor Lou heard Claire's statement.

They were still only in the entryway, the first section of the bottle home. Claire gawked at the ceiling, watching the octopi slide around on the top and sides, their radiance shining through.

As they moved into the first room of the home, Claire ran her hand over one of the boulder-like chairs, feeling its smoothness. She had never seen a boulder shimmer like a pearl. They must have been what the merfolk sat on. Claire wasn't too sure how comfortable they were, but they sure were exquisite. On one side of the room, by the boulders, there was a giant tree stump. It must have taken five very strongly built men to carry. But Claire was especially intrigued by all the daggers and tridents and swords displayed in the nooks and crannies of the wooden archways that stretched down from the ceiling. Their house was very minimally decorated, yet at the same time, to Claire, it was awesome. *Peculiar* but awesome.

"Follow us, Claire." Lou motioned to her as both he and Cora started forward. They must have been headed to where their dinner would be.

Claire didn't exactly want to follow them. She wanted to admire every single dagger and trident and sword that was displayed. She had never seen anything like them before. Blades crafted out of crushed shells and sea glass. They were so interesting to her.

As soon as Claire swam forward, a small stingray snuck around the corner of the archway. Luckily, she saw it, watching its actions closely. It appeared to be smoothing out the floor of sand and eating any small sea creatures in its path, like a live vacuum.

Cora and Lou came to a halt in the next section of their home, and Claire looked over to find another rock. It was much larger and jagged, looking as though it had just sprouted up from the ground. It spanned the size of an average kitchen table. Bunches and bunches of seaweed salad and stuffed-to-the-tippy-top oyster-looking shells were neatly splayed on the giant rock inside some weird bubbles.

"Why is the food in those?" Claire asked. She pointed to the makeshift table while tilting her head and pursing her lips. She started to slide onto the bench, a sort of seat that ran all around their interesting table. It was quite a tight squeeze, and oddly enough, she didn't get scratched by the boulder at all.

"You know how in the human world you have refrigerators?"

Claire nodded.

"All we have to do is store our food in one of these Zubbles, and it can be stored anywhere. As absurd as it is, these enchanted bubbles keep our food cold or hot, and fresh."

"Well, oh my, I don't know if I even want to go back to my world," Claire laughed, very much joking.

"You *can* live here," both Cora and her husband said at almost the same time.

"Oh, I was just joking. You were too, right?" Claire asked them.

"No, most certainly not," Lou answered.

"Oh, well, how could that even work? Humans don't live down here, do they?"

"Actually, we already have several humans in our community. All we have to do is perform a few spells and such, and you'll be living just like a mermaid," Cora informed.

"And not to mention the fact that you could switch back to having legs whenever you wanted," Lou added.

"Hm, well, that's very interesting." At that moment, Claire wasn't even considering it. It was *just a silly thought*. "I couldn't live with the fact of knowing that I'll never see my family again and the fact that it was my decision," she remarked, with a tear in her eye. She squeezed her lips tightly together, attempting to hold back the tears that were about to break free.

"It is a difficult decision to make, Claire," Lou stated. He slid onto the smooth, reclaimed wood bench that surrounded the *table*.

Claire glanced around the room once more, getting a better look at everything. What she assumed was a wedding photo of Coralia and Lou caught her eye. She couldn't have imagined Cora any more beautiful with her luscious maroon hair that flowed perfectly over her features and her blue eyes that were as bright as the sun and as big as life. As Claire scanned the picture, she admired Cora's snow-white tail embedded with various sizes and shapes of striking gold and silver gemstones.

After she saw that picture, she noticed that somehow, Coralia was even more stunning now. And Lou, Lou was a handsome merman himself. She studied their tight, wrinkle-less skin. They both really didn't appear much older than the day of the picture. Perhaps they used an aging spell, she thought, for their skin was flawless.

"I don't know." Claire laughed loudly. "That is a crazy, crazy decision to make." She couldn't wrap her head around the fact that she was sitting there talking to a mermaid and a merman. She couldn't believe their words. Who would? Claire still didn't exactly know if she was dead or dreaming, or if she should get out of there as quickly as possible or have the time of her life. "But—" she began and then stopped herself. What she really wanted to say was that it seemed like too big of an offer to pass up, but she didn't want to make them think that she may choose to stay.

"You've only got one life to live; remember that, Claire." Coralia looked as if she could see Claire's future.

Did they *actually* think she would stay?

"I'll think about it and let you know in the morning."

*Just a silly thought.*

"Good idea. Sleep on it," Lou said in between bites.

"Now, I must admit, I really didn't think that I was going to like this, but it's quite tasty." Claire had a look of pleasure on her face while pointing with her miniature trident fork to the seaweed salad that was in the bubble.

Coralia and Lou laughed.

"Um . . . I'd like to thank both of you," she glanced from Cora to Lou, "for . . . for everything!" she finished, her voice shaky.

"Oh Claire, we are happy to help!" Lou stated.

Once again, Claire was over-the-moon happy and more grateful than words could express, yet she was still scared half to death and confused. Her face could trick anyone, though. Calm, cool, and collected.

"I never did ask; how old are you, Claire?" Cora questioned.

"Sixteen."

"And now, who do you have on land?"

"My mother, father, brother, and my grandparents. More, of course, but those are the main ones." Claire gave a soft smile and nod.

"Are you the older or younger sibling?" Lou asked curiously.

"Older by three years."

"Lucky." Lou smiled mischievously.

"Extremely," Claire answered, a sly smile forming on her lips. She leaned back in her seat. Why were they asking all those questions? Were they simply just curious? Was it as innocent as that? Or was it more than that?

Something *evil?*

Claire didn't have much time to think or stress about the matter before they asked her more questions.

"Now Claire, do you work? Attend school?" Cora asked.

Claire smiled, but it disappeared quickly. Then she gently laid her tiny trident fork down on the boulder. "I do both. I work at my family's dairy bar, and I coach tennis for little kids." A very slight smile spread across her lips, but it was a sad smile. She tilted her head and focused on something through the small space that the octopi weren't covering, thinking back to a memory. "The dairy bar—it's named after me, actually!" She laughed but only slightly—sort of a half-laugh—a sad laugh.

"You must be the favorite child!" Coralia remarked.

"Just the first!" Claire shrugged. Her parents didn't pick favorites.

"What about friends? Do you have a lot of those up on land?" Lou asked. He must have been starved after a long day at work because boy was he piling the last of the food in quickly.

"No, not really." Claire looked quite proud of her answer. "I have a few, but I tend to stick to myself a lot. I like my time with myself. My alone time. I love knitting and writing poetry." She sure did smile big when she said writing poetry. "And . . . sketching. Sketching was what I was doing before I ended up here."

*Maggie's wedding.* After all Maggie had been through, Claire should be by her side. *She had to go back.*

"You know, you don't need tons of friends anyway. It sounds like you keep yourself occupied enough with everything you do."

Claire smiled and nodded once more. That was very true. "I really, really wish I could finish this, but I'm completely stuffed!"

"Oh, don't you stress it!"

Claire glanced at her watch. "Wow, midnight! It's getting late!"

"It's only seven down here."

"Goodness, five hours behind!" Claire yawned.

"Would you like for me to show you to your room now?" Cora questioned while raising an eyebrow.

"That would be nice." Claire smiled softly.

"Then we should get going." Coralia motioned toward the window behind Claire, an area where the octopi weren't latched onto.

Claire quickly turned and stared out of it for a moment, noticing that behind the bubble dome that they had come from, there was another similar one. It towered much higher than the clouded one.

It was much wider and more colorful too. Claire could only imagine its beauty until they got over to it and saw it up close.

After realizing that the stingray was just about to swim under the table, Claire quite literally fell out of her seat. *Phew.* That would have given her a scare if she had touched it.

"Bye, Lou!" she called out. She waved, and he waved back, grinning. Then they were out the door.

Once outside, Claire peered around in delight at the magnificent scene of lights. She noticed that Cora's house and her neighbors' houses formed a circle. A little group of homes. There was a house next to Cora and Lou's that was similar to the dome building. It was lit up like a Christmas tree by some sort of animal, just like Cora's home. But through the darkness, the glow of the animals was all that Claire could see. She imagined that if her home and her neighbors' homes were all gathered in a circle, too, it would be such a lovely view out her bedroom window when her neighbors decorated their homes with lights near Christmas time.

A few slightly lit structures sat off in the distance but certainly not in the direction that they were headed. Somehow, it was even darker than when she had arrived at Cora's house, so she could only see things that had lights on them. Some were insanely bright, like tons of flashlights tied together. Gleaming balls of light. What exactly *were* they?

Several feet away from Cora's house, Cora stopped suddenly and stuck her hand out in front of Claire, motioning for her to stop as well. Claire threw a concerned glance her way, but Cora's eyes were already shut. She looked as though she was waiting for something or someone. *Summoning them*. Claire kept her eyes on Cora for a moment. Suddenly, Claire heard whooshing sounds that were quickly growing louder and as she turned her head, she saw huge clusters of light rushing toward them on both sides, swirling all around, like bees around a hive. They were rushing toward them so rapidly that Claire could hardly focus on what they really were. She felt her heart begin to beat at an uncontrollable rate. Were they about to come and attack her? *No way*. She attempted to slowly swim off, but she was entirely frozen by fear. She couldn't physically even move a muscle. Again, she lost control of her own body. She felt her stomach begin to creep up into her chest like it often did when she was being whipped through the air while riding a roller coaster. She hated that feeling.

In the distance, near the bubble dome buildings, a lit path began to form. A magical pathway. Before

Claire could blink, the small starfish that had been swirling around her were now gleaming below her feet. Her jaw dropped. Now *that* was awesome . . . and spooky that Coralia could do *that much* with her mind and magic.

Cora nodded to Claire, motioning for her to move along, letting the lit path lead the way. That was *normal* to the merfolk.

Claire just shook her head in amazement, unable to stop gawking at the pathway below her. She looked up, not spotting many fish, but a few sea turtles swam past, over the illuminating pathway, leaving trails of tiny bubbles behind. They were giant and graceful, and shades of green Claire had never seen before.

Off the path, even though Claire couldn't see it well, there was what looked like a sewer cap that one may see in a parking lot. It looked as if it were trying to be *camouflaged. What is it used for?* It was the merfolk world, so it certainly wasn't being used for what it was supposed to be; Claire knew it. As the two of them ventured through the city, it was quiet, the eerie quiet that occurred right before a storm, which was nice and peaceful, *in a way*.

But Claire was still so very *hesitant* about it all.

They swam through the city the same way that they had gotten to Cora's house, except they had the pathway now. Claire couldn't get over just how cool it really was. But wasn't it cruel to all the animals that they summoned too? She didn't like that.

As they got to a large bubble dome that was as colorful as a rainbow, gleaming just like the pathway, Cora stopped quickly. It almost made you look twice. Its luminescence brightened the moment even more.

"This is it."

Claire was in a gaze. "Wow! This?"

The dome was smothered with sea creatures. There had to be thousands. *Tens* of thousands. Red, violet, orange and every other color on the creation of the earth made up the beautiful rainbow glow. The sea creatures were quite abnormal looking. Some of them looked like colorful mushrooms with eyes. Others looked like extremely large striped caterpillars. Each caterpillar-looking creature looked like a rainbow in itself.

Before Claire was able to observe it all, Cora started forward, right through a double door like the one on the first dome that Claire was in. The sea creatures shone down on them like the glow of neon lights. Quickly, Cora took a sharp left turn and there they were, at Claire's room. It all happened so fast, and even for the short time that Claire was in the quiet hallways of the dome, she felt welcomed.

Something told her she didn't need to worry about her safety. In a building filled with such serenity, what did she need to be concerned about? But at the same time, Claire didn't feel welcome there. Not because of anything the mers said or did, she just simply didn't. Truly, she didn't know how to feel about the whole situation—she didn't completely know what was happening.

The giant suite door had Roman numerals on it. Claire was pretty sure that the numerals were 172. Coralia slowly placed her one and only blue-painted fingernail in the small hole in the bronze door handle, and a teeny tiny crab crawled from inside the door handle, climbing onto her nail, looking as though it was studying her nail very closely and thoroughly. Seconds later, it disappeared back into hiding. Coralia removed her finger, and the door opened mysteriously, as if there was a ghost opening it, revealing the beauty behind it.

Claire's eyes widened and she let out a breath, relaxing slightly.

*Holy cow!*

"Now, I'd like to say that's the neatest thing I've ever seen, but I have a feeling that's just the start!" Claire giggled. "How does that even work?" She looked from the door to Cora, completely aghast.

"You see, guests get a fingernail painted. Each room has a designated nail polish color which contains a special ingredient, and when the crab senses it, it opens the door!" Cora remarked ever so casually. "For instance, this is the polish that you'll need to get in and out of your room." Cora quickly painted Claire's ring finger a cotton candy blue, and it turned out perfectly.

"Hey, thanks!" It was above Claire's head how Cora was able to paint her nail in the water and how it *actually dried* and how a nail polish and crab contraption could open a door.

"Here's your suite!" Cora waved her hand across the room.

Claire was shocked and thrilled by the beauty of it—the *luxury* of it.

"We try to make our suites for humans . . . well . . . more human." Cora chuckled.

*How* in the world did they get such luxurious, royal items? They didn't have *that much* to work with down there. Heck, it looked as though Claire had just stepped into a queen's quarters. She had never been somewhere so extravagant. She looked back behind herself. And to think she had just come from there. Sure, it was nice and all, but it was as if she had just stepped through that door to a whole different world—*a whole different century*.

She passed through the ray of moonlight that shone through the small skylight onto the pristine floor. Claire stopped, admiring the bed that was fit for a princess. The pearl-white comforter was fluffed up at the end by the polished, deep-gold footboard, and delicate lace hung off the sides. She dragged her hand across the smooth, cool surface of the giant rose-gold chest that sat at the foot of the bed.

*What is in there?*

She then looked up, focusing more on what she could see through the small patch of a window that the creatures left uncovered. Things out there moved leisurely. Lazily. And again, those crazy-bright blobs came into view. Still, they were far away.

*What are they?*

Claire's reflection bounced off the mirror closest to her and startled her. She turned to see herself in a Victorian, full-length mirror that was in the opposite corner of the room. *Phew*. It was just a mirror. The mirror reminded her of the headboard—intricately crafted. Elegant, blood-red roses were dangling off the sides. Were they real? Freshly cut? How? How had they gotten all the stunning pieces in the room down there?

Something hanging from the ceiling moved. Claire snapped her head toward it. She hadn't even realized that the ceiling was covered with hanging wisteria. Various lengths of lilac and crimson and pastel pink dangled above her. It sort of blended in with the sea creatures in a way.

*How did they get all of it?* She couldn't shake her curiosity.

Claire hadn't heard any movement behind her, so she looked back. "Cora, how come you're not coming in here?" she asked obliviously.

"Haven't you noticed there isn't water in there? I can't."

"Oh, I'm sorry, I didn't even think twice about it. I'm so used to not being in water that I really didn't even notice." Claire pondered for a moment. The water stopped right at the door where you enter the room, at the doorframe. The water, flowing in a circle, *looked* like an entrance to a *portal*. "And how does the water stop right here at the doorway?" She was very curious, moving to lean on the wall right next to the door by Coralia.

"A spell, magic, whatever you may call it. It's only stopped for human guests."

Was that how they got all the extravagant items in the room, too, by using their magic?

"Well, young one, you better get some rest. In the morning, I'll give you a tour."

"A tour?" Claire beamed. "Gee, thank you so much!"

Coralia gave Claire a wink and a slight smile. "Good night, Claire. See you in the morning."

"To you as well!" Claire called out merrily as Coralia shut the giant, heavy, ship door.

The door was the only thing in the guest room that truly reminded her of the sea.

She walked back over to the giant chest, crossing the royal, velvet rug. She felt its softness below her feet. She couldn't even remember when or where she had lost her shoes. It was probably when she was floating in the clouded waters.

Coralia hadn't said whether she was allowed to open the chest or not, but it would be locked if she wasn't supposed to, *right*? Claire felt like she *needed* to open it. Her curious mind led her to it. She tried it with one hand, but it just squeaked. Then she put more strength into the pull. It quickly sprung open. Claire gasped, her hands flying to cover her mouth. One gorgeous nightgown hung from the top of the chest and flowed into the bottom, poufing out and filling up the rest of the chest with its tulle. Claire quickly pulled it out, careful not to rip the delicate garment at the same time. She held it up to her body. It looked about her size too. Was it for her? It had to be. But *how?* Then she saw a little purple notecard tied to the velvet hanger. Her heart fluttered. She was going to be very disappointed if it wasn't for her.

*'Claire, twice a day, a new outfit will appear inside the enchanted chest.'* was inscribed on the pretty, purple notecard.

Claire was astonished. How exactly had it all been set up? How did they know her size?

*She wasn't so sure she wanted to leave.*

Next to the small, glass table beside the bed where some more roses were placed was a golden door with pretty, floral prints in all four corners. The bathroom?

Claire ran like a giddy child to the door, slowly opening it and peeking around. A candle-lit lamp sat on the pink quartz countertop, giving some light to the shadowy darkness of the night. Claire studied herself in the spotless mirror for a moment. She had just noticed that her hair was dry. *Magic.* She could only imagine the things to come. There was a hairbrush placed on the counter as well. It was so nice and new. It was wooden. Handcrafted. Precisely carved. Claire was too tired to brush her hair but certainly not too tired to change into the gorgeous, luxurious gown that was gripped tightly in her small hand. She looked down. Magic sure did fix everything or at least *almost* everything. Her clothes weren't gross at all, she thought, as she dropped them to the clean, glossy floor, eager to get the gown on. She slowly and carefully slipped it over her flushed body. It was cool against her warm skin. Satin-like. Claire slid her arms through the poufy armholes, letting the precious garment slide down her body. It was a cream color, lacey and frilly and fit for a princess.

Not her.

The whole place just wasn't her, but she liked it very much. The gown was much more comfortable than she assumed it would be. Claire stared at herself in the mirror once again. She tilted her head, almost laughing. She had never looked so fancy in her life, especially to simply go to sleep. Claire left the bathroom, the gown bouncing with every step she took. Then she slipped into bed—what she had been waiting to do since she first saw it. It was truly like a marshmallow, not too hard or firm but not too soft. She sunk down even further, pulling the warm, comforting, lush covers up to her collarbone, simply just thinking. She was amazed, to say the least. Claire patted her soft pillow, feeling like a princess on her throne, praying that it wasn't a dream, and then she drifted off.

# Clove

Groggy Clove quickly wrote about the dream or whatever the heck it was and then tried to go back to sleep. *I've got to tell Lucas about this. How? I'll have to meet up with him while Roman isn't home. But what if he finds out? He would have a death grip on Lucas if he were to,* Clove thought. She alternated between lying on her right side, her left side, and her back for close to an hour, before finally falling back to sleep.

She was woken up by her brother playing basketball around half past seven, the ball constantly pounding against the ground. Even though it was summer, she decided she would get up. She glanced out of her large, lace-curtained windows, and the bright light that shone through them nearly blinded her. Along with Roman was Lucas.

Clove walked downstairs, yawning and still half asleep. No one else was awake, not even the dog. She wasn't quite ready for breakfast yet, so she quietly snuck outside and watched the boys play for a few minutes. As Clove stepped out the door, she made eye contact with Lucas but broke it as quickly as it was made.

Yuck, it was already practically smoldering out.

"Morning, sis!" Roman called out in a bright, chipper tone.

Clove sneered. "Yeah, good morning to you too." She tried to make it very obvious that she was annoyed.

He raised an eyebrow. "Boy, someone woke up on the wrong side of the bed," she heard him say to Lucas and laugh.

"C'mon, give her a break; she just woke up." Lucas rolled his eyes and shook his head, annoyed as well.

Clove liked the fact that Lucas defended her, but Roman gave him a weird look and narrowed his eyes at him, giving him the evil eye.

"I'll be back in a few," Roman announced. He stuck his tongue out at Clove as he passed her; she rolled her eyes while doing the same thing back, then he went inside.

Lucas followed him up the porch steps and sat down across from Clove in their hammock. He tilted his head toward her, leaning in while raising his eyebrow. "So?"

"I had another one," Clove stated in almost a whisper.

"Another one of those things where you saw that girl?" he asked while searching her eyes.

She nodded immediately. "Yeah. Could—could we meet again?"

"Okay, uh, yeah, sure. My house? The park?" he asked. They talked quickly and in a very hushed tone.

"You choose."

"My house," he decided.

"We've got to plan for when Roman isn't home, though," Clove said. She pointed toward her house and grimaced.

"He told me he's taking his girlfriend out tonight, around six."

Clove could hear footsteps quickly moving toward the front door. "Can I come over then?"

"Sure thing," he answered quickly.

Her brother quietly and sneakily opened the door, glancing at them both. "What are you two talking about?" he questioned, mainly eyeing Lucas.

Instead, Clove answered. "Barbies and dress up!" she said with a poker face.

Lucas tried to hide his laugh.

Roman wasn't amused. "You're hilarious, really," he answered, giving that same poker face right back to her.

"Right? I really should be a comedian."

Roman rolled his eyes.

She was just so sick of him being so nosy.

"C'mon, let's go finish this game."

Lucas glanced back at Clove and mouthed, "See you later."

*Ugh, why does he have to be so charming and perfect?* Clove wondered as he walked back into the sun, which made his fluffy hair shine as he ran his hand through it, flexing his bicep slightly. Clove blushed, her stomach feeling as though butterflies were frantically fluttering inside.

Growing up, he was always the nicest to her. He was there for her if she had no one to sit with. He always included her and made her laugh. *Maybe he is just nice, or maybe there is a different reason for his kindness, and he is just waiting for the right time to show it. No*, that was just a hopeful thought. Clove's mind was wandering too much.

Clove's stomach began gurgling, and she figured it was time for breakfast. She slipped back inside and poured herself a bowl of cinnamon-raisin granola and sliced up an apple for herself, the granola giving the whole downstairs a slight cinnamon scent. Clove had never smelled granola with such a strong aroma. It was a new brand her mother decided to try. She was all about trying new things.

After breakfast, she returned to the kitchen and dropped her spoon in the dead silence.

*Crap.*

"Clove?" her mother called from upstairs, giving her a jump scare.

She hadn't realized her mother was already awake. "What?"

"Would you like to go out with me today?" Iris called back. "I'm going grocery shopping!" Her mother sounded way too energetic and excited for the early time that it was.

"Maybe, when?"

"I'll leave in about an hour if you want to go."

"We won't be gone all day, right?" Clove knew she told Lucas that she'd be at his house that evening and that her mother sometimes didn't always stick to her plan.

"No, just some light grocery shopping," Iris finally answered.

"I'll go."

Soon after that, she ventured upstairs to pick out an outfit—a pink tie-dyed shirt that said Florida on it in some squiggly print that she had gotten when they went there on vacation one fall. That was several years ago, so it was slightly small and tight, but she loved it too much to say goodbye, even if it was almost a crop top. To go along with that, she chose a pair of light wash jean shorts and her favorite fairy necklace. The necklace had belonged to her grandmother who had passed on way too early. Clove missed her greatly. On the back of the fairy, one of her grandmother's favorite sayings was etched; *'Failure is fine. 'Tis what we choose to do with ourselves after that failure, which truly matters.'*

Clove always wondered where her grandmother had heard that first. The necklace? Or somewhere else? It was so simple yet very true and easy to forget, especially when frustrated.

She finished her outfit with gold jelly sandals and simple, gold stud earrings in all four of her piercings.

Clove was in the midst of putting her rubbery shoes on when another Claire episode happened. First, she noticed how sandpapery her tongue was against the roof of her mouth. Then she couldn't see anything. She felt bottom heavy, unable to move a muscle.

Claire, fighting for her life in the water, trying to escape the container, flashed in Clove's mind. When Clove saw the mermaid, Coralia, her heart nearly stopped, and when she latched onto Claire's leg and started yanking, it completely shocked Clove. It was odd that she could see the mermaid and Claire couldn't. She didn't believe what she was seeing. Yet once again, there was a *sense* of *connection*. For a moment, she thought that perhaps it was trying to harm Claire. And within the blink of an eye, just like Claire, Clove saw bright, obnoxious, flashing lights and heard very loud noises, making her ears ring. Then everything went pitch black for a minute, like someone turned the lights off.

Clove could hear Claire moan in pain and saw Claire hold her leg momentarily. After the pain eased, she finally looked up, quite startled. Clove watched Claire and the mermaid converse. The mermaid didn't seem violent . . . yet. Clove tried to hold her laugh back as she watched Claire swim into the wall. After a few seconds, they started to swim away, right as it stopped playing in her mind. Now, Clove wished that she could see more, even just a glimpse, but she knew she would have to wait until the next one.

There would be another one. There always was.

Clove sat on her bed, thinking about everything she had just seen. She suddenly remembered that she was going to the store and still needed to brush her teeth. She undressed so she wouldn't get any toothpaste on her cute outfit and have to change. She certainly didn't want that. So, in her bra and underwear, there she stood, brushing her teeth. Over the hum of the toothbrush, she could hear footsteps coming upstairs, quickly moving closer and closer. *It must be mom,* or at least that's what she thought, what she hoped. The bathroom door practically burst open, and it was Roman. She gasped, her heart racing and her cheeks flushed; she knew they must have been as red as tomatoes. She felt as though she was about to faint from embarrassment. They both stared at each other for a split second. It was just different than him seeing her in a bathing suit.

He threw his hand to his forehead. "I'm so sorry; I should've knocked. That's all me." He displayed an awkward, uncomfortable expression.

Hadn't he heard the toothbrush or seen the light under the door? No, of course he probably hadn't. Like normal, he most likely wasn't paying any attention.

"Yeah, it is all on you. Please do next time!" she shouted, rage plastered across her face. Clove slammed the door hard in his face.

The event had happened before, but not in a few years. She had changed, and him walking in on her now was different. She wore a bra. And she didn't wear *My Little Pony* panties anymore. She was almost fourteen.

Thank God it wasn't Lucas, she thought to herself and laughed. Oh, how she would have been completely mortified.

She quickly finished and went downstairs, where she found her brother and, yet again, Lucas, but they hadn't seen her. She could hear them talking around the corner in the hall.

"That was . . ." Roman searched for words. "Awkward. Super awkward," he finally blurted out.

Okay, why did he have to tell Lucas about their little situation?

"That hasn't happened in years. She has really gotten older."

"She has, hasn't she? She's . . . pret—" she heard Lucas start to say, then quickly catch himself, flustered as he searched for something to say to cover his slip-up.

Her breath hitched in her throat, and her heart got all fluttery. Had she heard him correctly? If so, Lucas was very lucky Roman hadn't heard or hadn't been paying attention.

Clove had never been so happy to hear someone say she was pretty in her entire life. She was almost positive that was what he was going to say. A smile that stretched from ear to ear spread across her face, which she had to try to hide as she attempted to casually walk across the kitchen to grab a bottle of water to bring with her.

Boy, that took things to a new, interesting level.

How did Lucas mean that?

Roman glanced over at her but broke eye contact right away.

She tried not to make it weird, but she could feel the tension hanging in the air.

"Are you ready to go?" her mother called out as Clove snatched a bottle of water from the case on the sparkly-clean counter.

"Yes, I'll be waiting on the porch," she answered, forgetting how miserably hot it was outside. As she tried to book it past the guys, Lucas caught her eye.

"Where do you happen to be going?" he asked with a smirk. He turned on his stool to meet her eyes, searching them. He was sweaty from playing basketball, the sweat beading up in his hair. Both the boys were. They must have been taking a water break.

"The store, grocery shopping," she politely responded, trying not to make eye contact with her brother. She also tried to be short with Lucas so Roman wouldn't be on to them—so that he wouldn't strangle Lucas while Clove and her mother were gone. But how could she look away when he always had to look so good?

She could hear her mother's footsteps behind her. Heels. *Platforms.*

"Let's go," Iris said, practically pushing Clove out the giant double front door into the heat.

Her mother always looked so presentable. She wore a pastel sundress with some bleach-white heels, an initial necklace, some simple, gold hoop earrings, and what Clove had smelled so many times, her mother's favorite perfume, *Berry Divine.*

Why so fancy just to go to the store? Clove sort of laughed when she saw her mother's errand-running outfit.

The drive was quite quiet and peaceful for a few minutes until . . .

"So . . ." her mother's voice trailed off as she narrowed her eyes at Clove.

"What?" Clove could feel her heartbeat speed up. She knew that tone of voice.

"Why did you really go to Lucas's house a few afternoons ago?"

"Oh, just to ask him about Ro's girlfriend." She tried to sound honest and convincing.

"Why?"

"I just haven't ever met her and wanted to see if she was actually real. Which I found out that she is." Clove gave her mother an innocent smile while laughing it off.

"Okay?" her mother said while glancing at her suspiciously, not buying her act.

"What?" Clove asked again, annoyed.

"You know, now that you're almost fourteen, I feel there's something that should be discussed."

Clove wanted to jump from the vehicle right about then. Not because she was embarrassed that she liked—*or loved*—Lucas, but because she really didn't feel like having that talk. *At all.*

"Sweetie, I really don't want you to have a boyfriend until you are at least fifteen. I just know that you've always liked Lucas."

Clove felt her face flush and knew she wasn't doing a very good job at hiding her uncomfortable facial expression. Clove wondered if her mother actually thought Lucas would ever like her.

Her mother laughed. "I don't care if you like him; he's sweet. I've just known for years and years and figured it was about time to discuss the fact. He's almost three years older than you, you know!" her mother said.

Adjusting her tone, Clove tried to be cool and mature about it. "Oh yeah, I know. And I mean, three years, that's—that's a lot." Clove grimaced. She didn't like to think about that. "If it makes you feel any better, we both absolutely hated to lie at the table the other evening, but we knew that if Roman knew that we hung out, he'd freak," Clove explained. She held her breath, hoping her mother wouldn't be too upset.

"I don't blame you. He's a little too protective of you at certain times," her mother remarked casually. Then it hit her. She snapped her head Clove's way, focusing completely on her eyes. *That's where the truth was.* "Were either one of his parents home?" Iris questioned in a strong, serious tone.

Clove started to sink down into her seat. "No," she answered as her voice squeaked.

"Hm?"

"No, neither one of them were," she said loudly. Nervously. She shook her head. "I know, it was a stupid choice," Clove added quickly before her mother could say a single word.

Her mother bit her lip. "I'm glad that you realize that, and I am going to ask you to never do that again until you are much, much older," her mother finished, focusing on the road. Iris was definitely steaming inside, but she needed to brush it off. She made *stupid* mistakes *too*. And Iris remembered how her parents were super strict with certain things and how she snuck around behind their backs. She didn't want Clove to do that. She would simply 'suggest' that Lucas could come to their house, so she could keep a close eye on them. A *very* close eye on them. She knew banishment wouldn't do a single thing and would most likely only make Clove rebel and do what Iris did when she was younger. She shuddered. Iris certainly didn't want Clove doing any of that. Besides, it was Lucas. Out of all the teenage boys she knew, she trusted Lucas the most, not that that was saying much. She still knew what he was *capable* of.

"Why is Roman so concerned anyway?" Clove questioned casually, tilting her head toward her mother. It was her turn to attempt to pry some truth out.

"God only knows." Iris laughed.

Clove didn't believe that her mother didn't know. "You know, I'm supposed to go over to his house later on when Roman takes his girlfriend out, so . . ." her voice trailed off.

"Go ahead. Just please don't go in if he's home alone."

Clove practically jumped out of her seat. "Aw, really? Thank you, thank you, thank you!"

Her mom looked over and laughed. "May I ask why you happen to be going over there . . . again?"

"Well, um, we just enjoyed hanging out last time, and he invited me over today," she answered, staring at her mother with an innocent facial expression. *She lied.*

"Alright." Iris thought about how Clove was getting older, so she thought that maybe Lucas did simply just enjoy hanging out with her. But Iris also wasn't dumb. She knew how boys could be, and although Lucas was sweet and *charming*, she certainly didn't completely trust any boy around her daughter.

"And one more thing. Please—" Clove started, but her mom knew what she would ask.

"I won't mention a thing to Roman. I am as clueless as him to all of this." She winked.

"Thank you, Mom." Clove gave her mother a soft, sentimental smile.

"You know, Lucas can *always* come to our house."

"Okay. I'll mention it to him."

Her mother smiled.

Thankfully, the conversation would be over since they were at the store now. The parking lot was packed almost to the back, and the store was scattered with people, but they were successful at getting everything they went to the store for, except for apples.

*Apples? What store doesn't have apples?* Clove thought. Perhaps she was being a bit dramatic because they were her favorite, and she was disappointed.

They would have been in and out of the store in quite a timely manner if they hadn't bumped into Clove's mother's jabber jaw friend. Clove kept discreetly checking her watch, because she knew her mom would talk and talk and talk. Thankfully, Iris's friend got a phone call. She was nice and all, she just always had a *ton* to say.

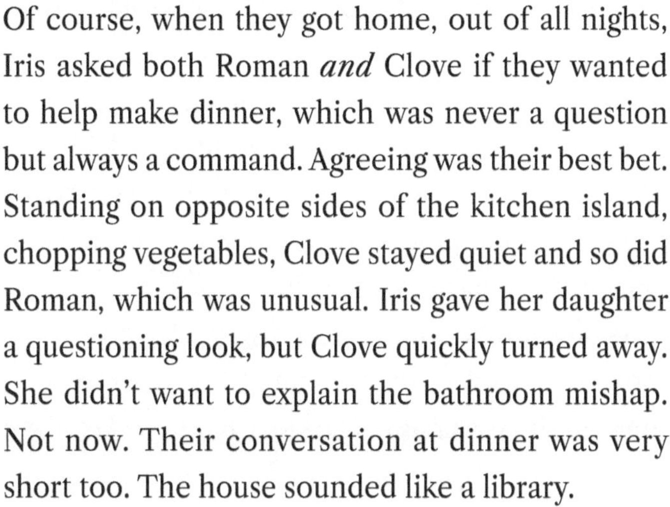

Of course, when they got home, out of all nights, Iris asked both Roman *and* Clove if they wanted to help make dinner, which was never a question but always a command. Agreeing was their best bet. Standing on opposite sides of the kitchen island, chopping vegetables, Clove stayed quiet and so did Roman, which was unusual. Iris gave her daughter a questioning look, but Clove quickly turned away. She didn't want to explain the bathroom mishap. Not now. Their conversation at dinner was very short too. The house sounded like a library.

Clove breathed a sigh of relief when her brother left to take his girlfriend out. She watched as the headlights on Roman's car flicked on as he backed out of the driveway, shining in her window. She sat in her room, eagerly watching the clock for a few minutes before walking over to Lucas's to make sure she wouldn't be caught by Roman while he was driving to pick up his girlfriend. Clove never knew if he *might* just *forget* something and have to turn around.

As Clove quickly walked down her driveway, she looked around, no longer seeing the sun in the sky.

The clouds hung low, casting many eerie shadows. Even though her mother was watching her from their porch, Clove made sure to keep a fast pace, not wanting to get kidnapped like Claire. She was very paranoid even when cars weren't around and it was dead silent, especially since she started seeing Claire in horrific situations. The silence made it eerie since she could hear every snap of a branch and every crunch of a leaf. Every time she heard something, she practically jumped out of her skin, her heart racing all over again.

As she hurried up his driveway, she could see the soft lights on the fountain just starting to peek through the water and sparkle. Unlike the last time she had been over, the gold SUV was in the driveway, which made her smile and turn all giddy inside. Unfortunately, the little, delicate flowers that were usually blooming so beautifully had already fallen to the ground, left to rot.

The smell of pumpkin pie blew through the air. It smelled like the scent was creeping out of the cracked window above the flowering plants. Lucas's mother, Candy, adored baking and often brought fresh-baked goods to Clove's family, which they loved. So far, pavlova was Clove's favorite because of how it melted in her mouth.

On the first knock, Lucas opened the door.

*Was he waiting for me?*

Luckily, his mother was home this time.

"Hi, sweetie!" Candy hollered from the kitchen.

"Go ahead, peek in there."

Clove smiled. "Do I smell pumpkin pie?" she asked excitedly and laughed.

"You sure do! I'm making one for your family and one for our family." Candy smiled. She was cleaning a mixing bowl, flour on her face, and her old apron tied around her waist.

"Awe, really? Thank you! We love your desserts!"

Lucas finally entered the kitchen, brushing up against Clove, giving her goosebumps, then stopped to stand by her. Clove could feel his warmth radiating off him.

Clove gulped. "Oh, by the way, my mom wanted me to let you know that if you want, we can hang out at my house," Clove mentioned.

He looked at his mom for an okay. She nodded.

"Actually, yeah, why not? Let's go."

"Stop by anytime you'd like," Candy shouted to Clove.

"Anytime? I might take you up on that offer."

They all laughed.

"Anytime!"

Lucas opened the fancy wooden front door like a gentleman and gestured for Clove to exit. "M'lady!" He laughed.

"Oh gosh, never say that again!" she jokingly yelled at him.

He laughed even harder.

 "So . . ." Lucas was trying to think of something to say. Anything. "How was your day?" he asked, looking down at Clove since he was much taller than her. He towered nearly a foot above her.

"Great, actually. Yours?" Her hands were latched together behind her back as she swayed back and forth while walking.

"I can't complain."

"Good, good."

There was a moment of silence. If it weren't for the frogs croaking and the crickets chirping, it would have been extremely awkward.

"Roman freaked the other night, so we really need to make sure he doesn't see us today." The tone of her voice made it apparent that she was nervous. And after Lucas almost completely slipped up earlier that day, she was a bit more on edge. Clove didn't exactly know what to think and hadn't been able to stop thinking about it all day.

"What'd he say?" Lucas's expression was uneasy.

Clove explained it all to him.

"I know he doesn't like me being around you," he stated in an irritated way.

"But why exactly?"

"Uh . . . you know, I'm not sure."

Clove knew that he was lying by his tone and the expression on his face. Something was going on.

"He was extremely demanding too," she added.

"Well, I partially understand his reasoning, but he needs to back away just a bit."

*He understands Roman's reasoning. What the heck is that supposed to mean? Does he mean he understands just because I'm Roman's little sister? Maybe one day the truth will come out; it always does*, she thought. But it didn't seem like it was going to happen anytime soon.

She changed the subject. Clove needed to focus on something else for a while, even if she just simply changed the conversation from one dilemma to another. "Anyway, I've seen Claire a couple more times," she told him as her house came into view. "Since I last saw you," she added.

His eyes widened. "Oh God, what happened now?" He tensed his jaw in frustration.

"Well, Claire was kidnapped, had a horrific car ride, was then thrown into a speedboat, accidentally thrown into the water, almost drowned but was able to break out of the container that she was in—"

"Oh my God!" Lucas chimed in, thinking that was all.

"Oh, I'm not done yet."

Lucas shook his head, raising his eyebrows in surprise, his mouth gaping.

"While floating in the ocean, she was pulled through what I assume was a portal . . . by a mermaid." She whispered that last part.

"Wait, hold on, I'm sorry, what? Clove, that's crazy!" he practically yelled.

"Shh." She quickly put her finger to her lips, laughing. "Someone might hear you."

"Sorry, just . . . that is absolutely insane!"

"I know. I'm starting to really freak out about this, Lucas."

Lucas began to speak, but Clove cut him off. "Wait until we get into my room." Clove didn't want to risk anyone hearing a thing about the situation.

Lucas nodded.

They had reached Clove's neighbor's precisely sculpted hedge, close enough to her house for someone to hear their conversation. And in the dimness of the night, you *never* know who may be lurking in the shadows.

Iris was swiftly walking up to the second floor as they entered the house, and she quickly turned her head toward them. A smile grew across her face. "Ah, you took me up on my offer," she said to Lucas.

"I did. Thank you."

"Mom, can we hang out in my room?" Clove asked her mother with puppy dog eyes, her heart pounding.

"Of course. Door open," she answered sternly. She was looking at Lucas as she said it, though.

"Thank you!" Clove smiled, her cheeks bright pink and warm from embarrassment.

Did her mother really think Lucas would try something with her?

Her mother gave her a slight nod, a smile pulling at the corner of her mouth.

When they got into Clove's room, Lucas stretched himself across her giant, bay window bench that looked over the large, foggy lake across the way. Clove, on the other hand, lay on her stomach on her bed with her chin propped up in her hands like a cute toddler.

Clove's lavender wall was barely visible behind all the pictures, similar to Lucas's room. A specific picture must have caught Lucas's eye because the next thing Clove knew, he was across the room. After carefully examining all the interesting pictures, Lucas looked down and said, "Cool lamp," admiring her purple wooden lamp with a butterfly carved into it. He then peered down to the minuscule nightstand that it sat on that had been her great, great grandmother's.

It was hard for Clove to wrap her head around how old it was. "Thanks."

"I guess I haven't been in here in . . . gosh, a long time."

"Probably years now."

"Jeez!" His eyes widened at the realization.

"So, do you know what could be happening with the Claire situation? Because I'm about lost!"

Lucas quickly pulled his phone out of his pocket and flipped it in his hand, showing off in a joking sort of way.

Clove raised an eyebrow. "Wow, impressive!" she joked, rolling her r while laughing.

"I—uh—did some research, actually," Lucas said. Then he started typing on his phone. "First, it said it could be a vision."

"I don't know, I don't think these are visions. Aren't visions kinda like seeing into the future? I mean, the car Claire was kidnapped in was a car from long ago. And the outdated clothes they wore—I just don't think these are visions."

"Yeah, I thought about that too. And then I read a bit about hallucinations just for the heck of it, but I don't think it could be that. Those are typically caused by a medication or a mental illness. And extreme sleep deprivation. Have you slept this month?" He looked up from his phone, smiling.

Clove giggled, trying not to blush at the classic Lucas Lynch smile. "Yes."

"No, but actually, are you sleeping alright?" Lucas asked in a tone that was more concerned than curious, like he truly cared.

She nodded. "Yes, Lucas." Then she gave him a soft smile.

"Okay. Good." He looked back down at his phone. "And then there are flashbacks related to reincarnation. There have definitely been some odd cases where people have claimed to have been able to see parts of their past life through dreams."

"But I'm having these things, whatever they are, in the middle of the day also. Like—these aren't only dreams while I'm sleeping."

"Exactly," Lucas said. "I only saw maybe one thing about people experiencing these daydream-like things, you know, like what you've been experiencing."

"Like flashbacks?" Clove asked.

"Yeah, like flashbacks, not just some random weird daydream about flying pigs."

Clove chuckled. "When I looked online, I didn't see much about flashbacks. Guess I didn't dig deep enough." She shrugged.

"There wasn't much, but I saw some people saying they were having these odd flashes of a scene, but from the past, which sounds like a flashback. They kinda said what you said; they thought it was their past life by the outdated items and whatnot that they saw." Lucas sort of scoffed at a thought he was having. "But what gets me is the fact that the first two times you had these things—"

Clove cut him off, "Flashbacks. Let's just call them that."

He nodded. "The first two times you had these *flashbacks* you were by the local park."

"Don't even bring that extra confusion into the mix," Clove ordered him.

He laughed. "Okay."

"I've thought about it too though," Clove confessed. "It is weird."

At that exact moment, her mother strolled past for about the fourth time in twenty minutes, eyeing both of them. Clove acted as if she didn't notice her, and Lucas continued scrolling on his phone. Luckily, Clove could see the reflection of the hall in her mirror, so she could see whenever her mother came along.

"Yeah," Lucas said, "it is."

"But what—what are the chances that I was *reincarnated*?" Clove looked down at her hands. "I mean . . . that'd be crazy. And . . . why are these flashbacks just now happening? Did being by the park just start triggering them for some bizarre reason?" Clove almost laughed at her own questions and thoughts.

All Lucas did was shake his head, staring off into space. "I have no clue. But if that's what's happening, that's pretty wild."

"Yeah it is!" Clove nodded, wide-eyed.

They indulged deep in conversation for many more minutes, their voices hushed as they watched out for Iris, and their conversation always circled back to the result of thinking that Clove was having flashbacks due to reincarnation. They couldn't exactly think of any other good explanation. In the teens' opinion, too much pointed to the flashbacks being reincarnation related. Talking everything over with Lucas gave her some piece of mind, but she was tired of thinking about it for the night. Things were getting quiet, and it was only about 7:30. For that day, they were both done brainstorming ideas of what it *could be*. Their brains had turned to mush.

"Do—do you want to watch a movie?" Clove was trying to be cool and casual but the squeak in her voice begged to differ.

He smiled and glanced at his watch while running a hand through his hair. "You know, that would be nice. When do you think Roman will be home though? He'll kill me if he gets home and sees us watching a movie."

"He usually stays out for three or four hours," she answered.

He nodded while calculating the time that they had.

"Popcorn?" Clove asked, eyeing Lucas while chewing her lip anxiously.

"What kind?" He mimicked her tone.

"Butter, cheese, sea salt, caramel, or dill pickle." She glanced out of her giant bedroom window at the shadowy lake, turning around just in time to catch a glimpse of the funny look Lucas was giving her. "What?" she asked, laughing.

"That was what, like, five different flavors you listed? Are you guys popcorn connoisseurs or something?"

That made Clove laugh harder.

"All those flavors and I still say butter. How about that?"

"Sounds good to me," she told him, attempting to suppress her lingering laugh. She turned on her heels to head downstairs to the quiet kitchen, Lucas following closely behind her. They passed by her parents' room. Iris was folding and hanging up laundry. She jumped slightly when Clove started to speak. "We're going to watch a movie."

Iris gave them an interesting glare. Lucas held in a nervous breath. She shot a 'you-touch-her-and-I'll-do-worse-than-her-brother-could-ever-do-to-you' look his way. He gulped and backed up even farther away from Clove than he had been.

"Okay?" Iris answered slowly. She was obviously surprised. But why wouldn't she be? She had expected them to hang out and talk or play board games. Watching a movie was a whole new level. Her baby didn't need to grow up so fast.

"Need any help?" Lucas asked when they reached the kitchen.

Clove glanced around the room quickly. The spotless, glass countertop sparkled as she flicked the light on, and the violet roses arranged in a crystal vase, which her father had bought for her mother, caught her eye.

Even though she was only almost fourteen, she desperately wondered if she would ever have the relationship her parents had. It was truly her dream, from the small, sweet gestures that meant the most, to the enjoyment her parents found in the simplicity of each other's company. She remembered finding her parents sitting in complete silence outside or on the couch when she was younger. She always wondered how that could be fun. How boring, she thought, until she began feeling that way around Lucas—finding peace in his mere presence. Every moment of it. Out of all her parents' time together, from the extravagant cruises to the daredevil experiences, they seemed most content while doing the most ordinary things: sitting in the kitchen snacking on chocolate, or weeding the garden together, or fixing a broken appliance, because really, truly, those weren't just the most ordinary things when they were in each other's company. Clove admired her parents' relationship. They had gotten together when they were slightly older than Clove and Lucas. They had Clove and her brother young but that never made them bad parents like most people *always* assumed. Her parents were different, but they were very involved, compassionate parents.

"I can't think of anything. Thank you, though. You can try to find a movie if you'd like," she offered casually after snapping out of her daydream.

He studied her for a moment, then grinned while flicking his thumbs up. As he headed to the TV room, his fluffy, wavy hair that suited him *so* well bounced with every step he took.

*What had she been thinking about?* He wondered.

The common questions that often came to her crept into her head as she watched him saunter away. *Will he ever like me? Or . . . does he already?*

No, she was just daydreaming. He was far too old for her. They would always just be friends. But what about his earlier slip-up? Maybe she had just heard wrong? Every time she thought about it, butterflies danced in her stomach.

Clove quickly ran to the bathroom while the popcorn was popping, and it stopped at the perfect time, beeping right as she stepped out of the bathroom. She grabbed two large salad bowls after climbing up on the counter to reach the stupidly high shelf. Clove sure could have used Lucas's help then. At last, she dumped the butter-coated popcorn into the large bowls, filling the air with a sweet, toasted aroma.

As she headed through the dark hallway, the large TV suddenly flashed and illuminated the wall.

Lucas gestured to the TV. "How about this?" he asked, sinking deeper into the chair.

Slightly embarrassed by what she was about to say, she asked, "What's the age rating?" She needed to make sure it was one that she was allowed to watch.

Lucas started scrolling to find it. TV-14 came up.

"Eh, that should be fine. Gotta break the rules sometimes, right?" Clove winked.

He shook his head and laughed. "A true rule breaker you are."

Her eyebrows curled up, and she nodded her head, looking extremely serious while handing Lucas his giant bowl of popcorn.

"Gosh, thanks! We could have just split one!"

Clove laughed, then plopped down on the far side of the comfy couch, far from Lucas.

The intro to the movie was weird. A woman, gazing at the exquisite summer sky, suddenly saw a gigantic drone flying around recklessly. It landed in her neighbor's driveway, and a famous band came out and started playing for her. Then a different woman was awoken from the wild dream by her obnoxious alarm blaring in her ears.

Lucas and Clove gave each other a strange look, weirded out by what they had just watched, then Clove giggled. Lucas looked foolish, searching for the TV remote, finally standing up and noticing that he had been sitting on it. He proceeded to pause the movie.

"Maybe you're living in a dream. Maybe all of this chaos is a dream," he suggested, laughing at his foolish statement.

Clove rolled her eyes while throwing popcorn at him. "Gosh! Why didn't I think of that? That *must* be it!" she said sarcastically.

Lucas smirked and tried to hide his quite noticeable laugh as Iris strolled by the room for the first time downstairs.

"Ah, you two will love that movie!"

"You've seen it?" Lucas asked, very surprised.

"Several times."

"Would you like to join us?" Clove asked, hoping her mother would say no for once.

"No. I'm going to finish what I was doing upstairs but thank you for asking."

*Yes!* Clove thought. She tried to hide her smile, but it didn't work very well. Clove blushed a bit. Thankfully, her mother walked away, acting like she hadn't seen her.

Clove was sure that her mother would be checking in on them every two seconds.

Lucas resumed the movie, *The Forest Lady,* and the two of them watched as the character who was dressed in an outdated style fixed an extraordinary breakfast of scrambled eggs, freshly picked berries, and homemade waffles, much more than the average person had time to make. To Clove, from the crisp, clear picture displayed across her TV screen, the movie didn't seem old at all. They panned out, showing that the woman lived in a tree house, in the middle of nowhere.

The two of them enjoyed the movie for a while longer until Clove heard footsteps in the hallway behind her. She didn't remember her mother passing by them again. And her father was still working. Clove slowly and cautiously peered behind herself and found her brother silently lurking in the shadows, watching the two of them. She could see the fury plastered all over his face. Rosie, their dog, was running toward him, wagging her tail. Clearly, Rosie didn't get the memo that it was not a good time for excitement.

Clove grimaced, panicking, while Lucas hadn't even noticed . . . yet. She could feel her heart beating against her chest like a racehorse's hooves pounding against the ground.

"What the hell?" Roman yelled out when they made eye contact. He threw his hands up in the air.

Lucas gasped.

"I can explain," Clove blurted out before Lucas even had the chance to make a peep.

*Famous last words.*

The room went completely silent as Roman rushed over and flicked the TV off, not taking his eyes off either of them. "So, what are you waiting for? Someone with a better explanation to walk through the door?" Roman asked, his eyebrows furrowed and arms crossed after waiting some time. His movements and expressions made it obvious that the fury was growing within him by the second.

"I'll explain," Lucas said. He stepped up in front of Clove, ready to take the blame. "I came over to see if you wanted to hang out but then remembered that you said that you were taking Evie out tonight—"

"That's crap, and you know it. And get away from her. Who do you think you are, her boyfriend?" Roman scoffed.

"Um, no?" Lucas stepped back a bit to be closer to Clove, shielding her from what may happen. Roman took another step forward, rolling his shoulders back and planting his feet hard against the floor. Lucas was worried that with Roman in a rage, he might try to hurt Clove. Normally when Roman got mad, he wasn't one for violence, but he looked crazy mad this time. *Furious.*

Clove began to think there was more to the story than she knew. It couldn't just be, *she is my little sister, so you two can't hang out.* There *had* to be more.

"I told you that I don't want you two hanging out," he added before another word was spoken.

"You're right, you did, and I listened for a while . . . but then I remembered that you're not her parent. And if your parents are okay with it, then who's to say otherwise?" Lucas answered with a smug smile, knowing that when Roman heard that, he would be boiling.

All Clove could do was stand and watch. It was as if she physically couldn't move, like she was trapped in her own body. What had gotten into Roman? *Drugs?*

"Who—" Roman started, when he was interrupted by their mother, who could tell that the room was heated.

Roman's back was to her, so she couldn't see how enraged he was just yet.

"What's up in here?" she asked with a bubbly attitude.

He snapped his gaze her way. Iris's eyes widened, and she raised her eyebrows so high. Oh yeah, he was mad for sure.

But then Roman relaxed his shoulders. "Nothing," he mumbled.

"Okay, well, Roman, would you just come here with me for a minute? I want to get your opinion on something." Iris was not always good at keeping her emotions out of her voice, and Clove could tell by her mother's tone that she heard the whole conversation and most certainly didn't have a single thing to *get Roman's opinion on*; she simply wanted to remove him from the situation.

Clove couldn't help but smirk at Roman, for someone needed to set him straight. He gave both Clove and Lucas a vile stare before venturing off to his mother's room, disappearing into the darkness of the second story.

Clove sighed. "I can't even begin to explain how sorry I am that you just got treated like that."

Lucas shook his head. "No, no, don't be. This is not your fault at all, not even the tiniest bit. You hear me, Clove?"

She just nodded.

"I know, but you guys are really good friends, and I don't want you and me hanging out to ruin that. I don't want him to hate you, but I think he might already." Clove talked in a quiet tone with tears sitting in the corners of her eyes, ready to escape down her cheeks at any moment.

"It's alright, okay? Seriously. Everything will return to normal . . . eventually." Lucas's voice was so soothing, like he could have said anything in that moment and it would have calmed her. "At least I hope," he mumbled.

Thankfully, Clove didn't hear that last part.

"I don't know what your mom is gonna say to cool him down." He laughed slightly. *Nervously.*

"I don't really think that she will change his mind. . . at all." Clove grimaced. "But just know, no matter what, I'll still hang out with you!" A smile started to appear back on her face.

"How about we go back to the movie? Forget about what happened for a while."

She nodded. It would lighten the mood. "Okay." She was sitting there with Lucas, her forever crush. She wasn't going to turn down just a few more minutes with him.


Not long after they resumed the movie, Clove caught Lucas glancing at his watch. "Got to go?"

"Yeah, I should probably head out, but let's finish this soon. Maybe we could uh . . . even finish it with Roman!"

They both burst out laughing.

"Oh, heck no!" Clove exclaimed.

Lucas started to walk out when he quickly turned back, locking eyes with Clove. There was barely any light in the room yet sparkles still danced in his eyes.

"Forget something?"

His lips parted, and he stayed like that for a moment. "No, but—" He took a long, deep breath. "Could I get your number or give you mine? I don't want that to sound weird but just so that if—I don't know—if you need something you can get a hold of me quicker. You know, quicker than walking to my house," he said, holding his breath.

Clove had tried to hide her smile—had tried to be patient and wait for him to finish his sentence.

Wow, he said that all in one breath and fast.

"Uh yeah, absolutely!" she burst out excitedly and gave it to him immediately.

Well, that made things a whole lot more obvious. *Maybe.*

"Thanks!" he exclaimed. "Have a—" he paused for a few seconds, scratching his head, thinking, "decent night," he finished, with a nervous laugh and half smile.

"Yeah, thanks, I'll try."

He waved. "Good luck." Then out the door he went.

Clove let out a sigh. Wow, that was a lot to wrap her head around. And what was so important to Roman that made him want to keep Lucas away from her that badly? Should she really *not* be around him? Was there something that her mother didn't know about Lucas? Clove couldn't imagine him doing anything too drastic. Lucas was Lucas.

*What has gotten into Roman?*

And was something going on between her and Lucas? Was it just her imagination? Of course it was, right? He was *just* simply *nice*. And why the heck was she getting all these flashbacks?

After a while, she got tired of sitting on the couch and running through her jumbled thoughts about everything over and over again, so she decided to hang out in her room. The confrontation was much louder there, going on for many minutes, yet it was still muffled.

Then suddenly, like the flick of a switch, all rooms went quiet. Clove heard her mother's door open. She looked up from the research she was doing on her laptop, realizing how heavy her eyelids were getting. Her door was slightly cracked, so she could see her brother quickly scurry past, heading to his room. Clove was then able to comfortably sink into her bed under her giant blanket and read her long-awaited book since everything was silent. She hated reading in anything but silence. She wanted to get lost in the mystical worlds for a while. She just wanted to kick back and relax.

But not long after she began reading, Clove started to feel as if she was going to pass out, and her vision spiraled into a black haze. *She knew that feeling.* This was not the mystical world she had hoped to get lost in. She saw Claire and that mermaid, Coralia, swimming through an extremely large and long hallway, the place that had many uses, as Cora had told Claire. Clove couldn't believe what she was seeing. She saw something that Claire definitely didn't, a human with her hands bound to the ceiling in one of the rooms. She was inside an odd half bubble that was bulging from the wall. Clove's breath hitched in her chest and her heart picked up speed. *Oh my God.* Were they going to kill her? The woman didn't look the least bit worried or in distress, though. *Odd. Disturbing.* Clove turned her focus to the woman's feet, where iridescent scales were beginning to grow, creeping up onto her legs. Maybe it was by choice? Clove could only hope, but the scene wouldn't stop playing in her mind. She wanted to shake Claire and ask her if she was crazy for going with that mermaid. But since Claire hadn't seen that, they just kept moving along. No questions asked. Clove had no other choice but to do the same. She had to turn her attention away from the fact and focus on the good—Claire was still alive . . . *for now.*

Clove saw the ceiling in the fanciful hallway, and her hand flew to her mouth. The flowing flowers were fabulous. Clove imagined touching one. The tiny petals would feel like silk, she thought. She could *almost* smell the sweet aroma.

At several points, Claire wondered if she had gotten herself into a mess, but they continued venturing through the hall. At last, they finally reached the door, the woman in the bubble still fresh in Clove's mind. *Haunting* her. The door to the outside—it was like a giant, double version of a door to a hobbit hole.

Clove was very curious as to how the dome over their world worked. Could people see into the merfolk world? When she looked back down, everything came into focus. It was extraordinary! A turtle would have practically touched Clove if she were there in reality. Clove and Claire were in awe at how brightly illuminated Cora's house was. *I could get used to this*, Clove thought.

They entered the colorfully decorated house. It was peaceful inside, no brother screaming or a dog barking, plainly peaceful; it was so nice. Clove watched as they all conversed. Everything was so extremely real. As Clove watched Claire eat the seaweed salad, it reminded her of the time that she tried it and hated it. She wondered how it was even possible to like it.

When Lou and Cora brought to Claire's attention that if she wanted to, she was perfectly capable of living in the merfolk world, Clove firmly shook her head, grimacing. *No, no, no.* To her it sounded like a dangerous, disastrous idea and while at the same time, she couldn't believe she was thinking it, *a great one.* Mainly dangerous, though. Life-threatening.

So many thoughts flooded both of the young girls' minds.

After the dinner that Claire was surprised she enjoyed, Claire and Coralia ventured off to Claire's room for the night. It was a short distance away from Cora's house but close enough if there was an emergency. Clove heard Claire ask how the dome covering their world functioned.

"There are several layers, sealed with potions," Cora told her. "Although we can see out, nobody can see in, in most areas, that is. The possessed merfolk and pirates have somehow found them and learned how to break in; however, that doesn't happen very often," Cora informed Claire.

"Will they try to hurt your kind?" Claire asked.

"They will. They come and battle for our jewelry. Thankfully, we have many forms of protection to help defend ourselves."

"Wha—what do you do with the intruders?" Claire asked quietly. She wasn't sure if she wanted to know the answer to that.

The flashback was getting slightly foggy, but Clove could still see okay.

"I'm sorry, Claire, but that is highly classified information," Coralia remarked quite secretively.

Claire gasped.

"What, is something wrong?" Cora asked in a sympathetic tone.

"No, no, sorry, not at all. Just—I—wow, that building—it's . . . stunning!" Claire burst out with much enthusiasm as she stared, catching her breath. She gawked in awe.

The different animals that created the privacy shield over the dome building were of various colors. It looked like a pastel rainbow threw up on it. Cora smiled at the joy that it brought Claire.

They floated in place for a short moment while Claire's jaw was ajar in astonishment, then continued toward *HoTail Merfolk.*

"Welcome!" Coralia cheerfully exclaimed.

Claire grinned, adrenaline pulsing through her veins.

"Follow me." Cora politely gestured toward a long, clean hall. Claire followed behind, attempting to keep up as speedily and nimbly as possible. But she was sure that she could be compared to a flailing whale.

There were whimsical doors scattered everywhere, even on the ceiling. Mysterious etchings covered a vast amount of them. Where did they all lead? Were they *all* suites? They took a quick left, and after a few doors, finally arrived at Claire's suite.

Clove and Claire's eyes widened at the genius nail polish crab invention.

And yet again, Clove saw something that Claire and Coralia certainly didn't. At the very end of the hallway, a tall, shadowy figure swam past in the blink of an eye, but it was as if it were a ghost mer. It didn't look like the rest. It was almost translucent. And he or she was much, much taller than Coralia.

Clove turned her attention away from the ghost mer right when Claire was learning how the nail polish invention worked, shaking her head slightly. Clove was over-the-moon amazed at such a concept. Cora pulled a funky, magical-looking bottle of the polish out of a hidden pocket in her tail, a random hole that appeared in her tail, and painted Claire's ring fingernail. It dried within a few seconds, which amazed and bewildered Clove since they were in the water.

The suite was brilliant! Extravagant! *It keeps getting better and better*, Claire thought. *And somewhat weirder and weirder at the same time with its princess bed and gold galore and magical chest.* Neither of the girls felt even the tiniest bit like they were still in the merfolk world when they saw the suite. How in the world did it all get there? Clove would lose her marbles if Cora said "magic" or "spell" one more time to answer Claire's questions. There was no way that it all was simply just the effect of magic or a spell, *right*?

Claire finished exploring her room; then exhaustion hit her. She felt somewhat safe and went to sleep in her oh-so-stunning nightgown, the glowing creatures around her dimming their light as her eyes shut.

"Clove?" Iris poked her head into her daughter's room.

She looked up with a curious expression, glancing at the time on her computer. Gosh, almost *five* minutes. Clove couldn't believe how long the flashback had been.

"You shouldn't have to worry about Roman giving either of you a problem anymore, at least I hope," Iris told Clove, seeming tired. Her eyes were a bit droopy.

Clove shrugged her shoulders. "Thanks for trying, but I'm sure he's still going to act ticked whenever Lucas and I hang out, and he'll make it quite obvious that he is."

"Well . . ." her mother's voice trailed off. "He knows that he is not your parent, so I'm hopeful that he will start acting like it."

Clove nodded, and a moment of silence passed. She didn't have much confidence in Roman quitting.

"I'm getting tired; I love you, sweetie. Good night," her mother said lazily, slowly closing Clove's door.

"Love you too, Mom. Thank you. Good night," she said through a half smile.

# Claire

As Claire awoke with a stretch, she glanced at the fancy, polished clock. *4:57 a.m.* She knew that meant that it was almost ten o'clock in the human world. She looked around, rubbed her eyes, and smiled. She was in the same place. Maybe she wasn't just dreaming after all. But gosh, was she tired. Claire attempted to go back to sleep but there was too much ruckus that it wasn't even worth trying any longer.

*Does anyone know what sleep is?* She stumbled her groggy self over to the giant lace-curtained window to try to make out what the noise was.

Confusion and concern hit her when she spotted a small jet floating in the work area. A few mers were gathered around it.

*Am I dreaming?*

From what Claire could make out, it was completely undamaged. Someone peeked out of one of the minuscule windows with a disturbed and frightened expression on her face, looking almost as if she were drunk. The woman's hair was a ratty mess that smothered her face, and her head bobbled back and forth. Claire couldn't think of one reasonable explanation for a plane to be underwater, especially in the merfolk world. She longed to still be wrapped up in the covers of the giant bed that was so cozy, warm, and fluffy. But curiosity kept her up.

Had the pilot lost control and crashed into their dome? *No.* It appeared too untouched to have crashed. It would have been in bits and pieces if it had crashed and broken through their dome. She just shook her head in frustration, lifting her hands to her temples, attempting to come up with some reasonable explanation to please herself, but she had nothing.

*Doesn't everything that enters need to come through a portal?* She was at a loss. In fact, she didn't want to think anymore; she wanted to sleep peacefully for another hour or two, have her tour, then make one of the biggest decisions of her life. Claire wanted so badly to be able to make that life-changing and possibly threatening decision, but it felt rushed. And it most certainly was. When she had gotten there just the day before, she had the mind-set of spending the night, touring the following day, then leaving to return to her life. She had her brother's birthday gathering to go to. And then, even though it was far in the future, Maggie's wedding. As insane as it sounded, she, in a way, wanted to stay. Claire constantly felt connected to the merfolk world—to the merfolk.

It was also 5 a.m., so she thought, perhaps, she was just tired and delusional.

She watched merfolk quickly remove the humans from the plane. Seven of them. Three women and four men, each escorted to somewhere that was not in view to Claire. To her, almost all of them looked asleep. *A spell? What is happening?* Thoughts ran through her mind as she continued watching extremely carefully. Suddenly, within the blink of an eye, the plane vanished as if it were never there to begin with. Not a single soul was near the plane when it vanished either. All the evidence was gone. The water didn't even bubble.

How could she sleep now, after seeing all of that?

She burst open the guest room door and practically flew out, forgetting that water was outside the door, as it slapped her in the face. A very unpleasant moment. She was more than eager for answers, though. When Claire exited the suite building, venturing out into the big world, she hadn't noticed anything out of the ordinary or off since the day before. She peered across the way. Cora's house and her neighbors' homes were perfect, looking in tip-top shape, except Cora's bottle home wasn't completely covered with sea creatures anymore. Now, only a line of them ran across and over toward the back. It looked so pretty with the light shining through the top, and the water was even clearer than the night before. It was very busy now. Mers were working and doing all sorts of miscellaneous tasks. They were everywhere, and Claire couldn't focus on just one. She glanced to the side, and now that it was slightly brighter out, she could see the several towering caves very well. Openings to black holes. *Where do they lead?*

A merman with the blackest of hair swam past her, catching her off guard and giving her a quick look up and down. His eyes told her that something was wrong, something with her specifically. She slowly peered down, finding her gown was bunched up to just above her belly button. Claire felt her face go red. Quickly swiping at her gown was her solution to getting it to flow below her knees again. The merman just smirked and laughed slightly, swimming off toward the caves; the other side of their city. He was one handsome fella too.

After a minute of being purely stunned, Claire was finally able to move. She didn't know if it was wise to venture outside the building alone. She didn't want to find out the punishment for snooping around and seeing something that she wasn't supposed to. Still, Claire did it anyway, with the bit of spunkiness that was in her.

She felt the workers knew what she would ask by their facial expressions as she swam toward them. "What just happened?" she demanded.

Claire was swimming in a really funky way, holding her gown down and trying to paddle at the same time. She hardly cared about the scene she was making or that all the workers were simultaneously noticing her clothes were a bit see-through. *Who cares*, she thought. *Merfolk practically live their whole lives half naked.* Her undergarments were like a bathing suit anyway. They'd all seen that before. She was sure of it. She was on a mission. She *needed* answers.

They all looked at each other, clueless for a few seconds as to what to say or perhaps what not to. "It's a long story. Why don't you ask Coralia later this morning? She was planning on telling you anyway; she just didn't expect you to see it," one merman stated.

Claire didn't trust them enough to wait until later. *What if they wipe my memory,* she thought, worried. *By later this morning, they could wipe my memory, return me to land, and I wouldn't have a single clue of what happened.* Claire thought long and hard about it. No, she wasn't going to wait. She shook her head abruptly. "No, I'm not waiting until lat—"

She was caught off guard by the young, handsome mer who swam up. Well shoot, her outfit certainly made everything a little embarrassing now. *What is it with all the mermen being so attractive?*

"Cora lives in that house," he informed Claire in his deep, mysterious voice. "If you are so eager, go ahead and knock on her door now. I can even bring you over if you'd like!" he added, gesturing toward her house as he held his arm out to the side.

Claire immediately found him to be a bit rude and short with his words, yet she still found herself becoming lost in his magical, deep blue eyes. And she knew she allowed her eyes to linger over his airbrushed like abs for a moment too long. Though his hair was dark brown, Claire assumed it was maybe a dirty blonde out of water. *Has he ever even seen his own hair out of the water?*

Claire finally found her words. "Thanks, but I know my way." She started to turn away but felt warm fingertips on her bicep. That definitely caught her attention, her breath hitching in her throat. He lightly pulled her arm back.

"I'm Hudson, and I'm sorry, what did you say your name is?"

"Claire," she replied in a dreamier tone than intended, yet it was very clear that she, too, was irritated.

His eyes grew wide when she said her name and he seemed slightly shocked and flustered, but then he gently shook her hand. His touch was the first thing that brought her any feelings of home. Of safety. "W—well then, Claire, pleased to meet you," he managed to say as he searched her eyes.

"Yes, it's—it's nice to meet you as well." She hardly finished her sentence before she turned around to head to Coralia's home, leaving Hudson staring at her from behind. In Claire's opinion, he was the most handsome and dreamy guy. *But he is a mer.* She was starting to get ahead of herself now. She didn't need to get sidetracked.

She quickly swam over to Coralia's home, her head cloudy and full of questions and thoughts. Then she harshly knocked on the solid door.

Just as she was about to turn away, Coralia answered. "Claire?" She paused for a minute, the water flowing through her hair as it normally did, making it nearly impossible to look messy. It was obvious from her groggy eyes that she had been sleeping. Confused, she invited Claire in.

Claire hated, absolutely hated being rude and barging in like that, but she didn't at all trust going back to sleep. She had no idea how Coralia slept through all the chaos.

"Oh, sit, sit. What's the matter?" she asked through a yawn. "It's only five-fifteen." She invited Claire to sit in the living area for the first time.

Claire was right; the boulder chairs weren't very comfortable. She had to strap herself in, unlike the wood bench where they had dinner the night before. *Maybe they are better for the merfolk since the merfolk have tails? Perhaps their tails add a lot of padding?* Once seated, Claire didn't beat around the bush; she got straight to the point. The image of dreamy Hudson was still sitting in the back of her mind. "Why was there a plane out there? And why were they dragging people out of it? You said that it is safe here," Claire raised her voice slightly, her hand shooting out toward where the plane had been.

Cora sighed. "It is . . . to an extent. I was going to get to that when I gave you the tour, but now could work too."

Just what Claire had hoped.

"As I mentioned earlier, at certain areas and heights, you can see into the dome, and recently, planes have started flying at those heights in those certain areas. So, therefore, the humans on the planes can see into our dome. That means they can see us, our world, and we don't want that at all! So, we designed detectors for when they fly at that certain level in those areas. It sucks them through a portal and puts them right there," she said as she motioned out the window that allowed for a gorgeous view of their world.

The bubble domes and all the other odd structures stood tall. There were trees, but they were mere sticks and seemed out of place. *When did trees start growing at the bottom of the ocean?* That would be a question for later.

Claire was speechless, trying to let all of it sink in. Was Cora serious?

"It also injects a potion into the plane to—to make the passengers sleep," she added. Claire grimaced. Cora could tell by Claire's face that she was quite concerned. Cora had a feeling that she knew why. Who wouldn't be worried after hearing that?

"The potion is not at all harmful."

"And what do you do with them?"

Coralia took a deep breath. "We give them a choice between living here or . . ."

Anxiously, Claire raised an eyebrow as Coralia paused. *Can what they do really be that bad?* "Or what?" Claire begged.

Cora bit her lip, shifting in the free space she had in her seat. "Well, you see, if they decide that they don't want to live here and that they want to go back to the human world, we wipe their memory."

"That's exactly why I wanted an answer immediately," Claire said sternly. She slapped her hand to her thigh and let out a huff.

"What? Why?"

"Because I thought that could have been me if I had gone back to sleep. I couldn't wait until later for answers. I thought that if you knew that I had seen that, that . . . well . . . that you'd immediately erase my memory."

Cora's eyebrows wrinkled together, and she pressed her lips straight, shaking her head immediately. "Absolutely not; we always give you a choice, except . . . well . . . if you decide to go back to land, we don't really have a choice whether or not to erase your memory. We can't give anyone a choice on that. It's too risky and threatening to us."

Claire sighed in relief, but she still wasn't exactly thrilled with Coralia's answer.

"Would you like for me to give you the tour now?" Cora asked through another yawn while fiddling with her life-like sea turtle earring.

"Why not!" Claire happily exclaimed. "If it's convenient for you, of course," she added while smiling at Cora.

Coralia leaned in toward Claire. "I make time for what's important."

Claire certainly wasn't going to say no to a tour of the merfolk world! She might have still been scared half to death and skeptical about the whole ordeal, but *no* was not going to be her answer. She needed to take advantage of the time she would be down there because it was not going to be long. And she never knew what may occur.

"So, where do we start?" Claire inquired, wide-eyed.

"Most likely the market." Cora paused. "Mainly because I need groceries."

They both laughed.

"I'll show you all around, including the Sand Way!"

"Sand Way?" Claire shouted out, hoping that she hadn't woken Lou. She gave Cora a confused, crooked glance. "What's the Sand Way?" she asked in a lowered voice, chuckling under her breath.

"It's a whole other world down there, Claire. A very lively tunnel system beneath us. We are full of surprises . . ."

"I'm starting to notice that!"

"Just give me about ten minutes, then we shall head out."

Claire longed to catch sight of Hudson again, so she informed Coralia that she would wait outside for her. Cora nodded and swam off through the archways in her house, disappearing into one of the side rooms.

"Stay close!" Coralia shouted from the unseen room as Claire was about to slip out the door.

"Don't worry, I will!" she shouted back excitedly, then proceeded to slip out of the massive trap door-like exit. Claire was a bit weary, but her adrenaline and enthusiasm for the adventure kept her awake. She peered about but didn't spot Hudson anywhere just yet.

She had never really been interested in anyone before. She was never eager to be in a relationship and never imagined herself in one. But there was just *something* about *him*. *He is probably married and has miniature Hudsons of his own*, she pondered.

Several workers scrambled around, yet Claire had no clue what they were doing. A few of them did look familiar to her from earlier.

Claire looked down. *Shoot.* She needed to change. She quietly opened the door and swam back into the living room area of Cora's home. "Cora?" she called out in a very hushed tone, peering around, trying her best not to wake Lou if he was sleeping.

"Yes?" Coralia floated out from around the corner that she had earlier disappeared behind.

"I'll be back soon. I forgot that I must change." Claire chuckled as she poufed her gorgeous gown out in front of her like a giddy child in a princess dress.

Coralia nodded. "Okay. You go ahead and do that." She smiled, knowing that Claire would love the outfit that the chest held.

Claire had never swum so fast in her life. She was back over to the suite in what seemed like a matter of seconds. *Goodness.* Talk about adrenaline. She had even forgotten to look for Hudson on her way. Not that she exactly wanted to bump into him while still in her half see-through gown.

She burst back through her door, not even waiting for it to magically, slowly open, practically crashing to her knees from the sudden change of being in water to being in none at all. Luckily, she was able to somewhat catch herself on the bed. It sprung her upright. And she couldn't get that chest open quickly enough.

This time, a bathing suit dangled from the top. That was so much better than regular clothing. At least it wouldn't fly up as she swam. It was a one-piece with shorts made of a stretchy, sparkly sort of material that was mostly maroon with a white zipper that ran from her collar bone to her lower chest. There was a dainty, white lace trim at the very bottom of the suit.

Claire snatched it up. *It was perfect.*

Again, it looked as though it was made just for her. She looked around the room, thinking, bewildered by the enchanted chest.

Wow, when had all the sea creatures removed themselves from the outside of the dome? While she was gone? Before she left? Had she been so flustered before she left that she hadn't realized? No way. She would have noticed how crazy bright it was. It was a never-ending skylight. But she didn't have time to admire it right then and there. She needed to change. She slipped into the bathroom, glancing at the oh-so-welcoming shower. Oh, how Claire longed for a hot shower. Even if it was only a quick rinse.

*No, no. Stay focused. Fight the urge.*

Claire quickly slipped the delicate gown off over her head, placing it on the cool, clean counter, careful not to rip or dirty it. Then she practically jumped into the bathing suit, squirming all around, trying to get situated. When she finally did, it fit like a glove. It was definitely her style. But she only got a quick glance in the mirror before she left again, leaving the gown behind, bursting back out of the suite, and heading back over to Coralia's home.

She swam a little slower this time, remembering she needed to save some of the small amount of energy and strength that she had for the tour.

There was no sight of Hudson.

*Why can't I get him off my mind?*

Then she peered straight ahead at Cora's bottle home. Right as Claire reached the house, much sooner than expected, Coralia swam out of the door. *Perfect timing.*

Cora looked up and met Claire's eyes. "My, that was fast!"

Claire chuckled.

"Well, are you ready for an adventure?" Coralia asked Claire, a little too energetically for six in the morning.

"I sure am!" Claire grinned from ear to ear; then they were off.

Claire admired the cleanliness of the powdery-white sand. She felt as if she could see for miles through the crystal-clear water. All of the houses had much character. One house that Claire passed was an old ship that had been restored to be a beautiful home. From the outside, it looked like most ships: round windows that were divided into four with thin wooden pieces, and dark-stained wooden planks to create the ship's shell. She knew it had to be beautiful on the inside. It looked as if it had been a luxurious ship at one time. A dark brown, intricately carved door was attached to a cave-like entrance that Clove assumed was another home. She imagined their living area must have been buried deep in the sand. Then there were some dome houses. Homes were placed oddly, just scattered throughout the town. And there were tons of those stick trees. *Why are they like that?* Then it hit her. The extremely bright light that she had seen off in the distance the night before must have been those trees. *But what was making them light up?* She got sidetracked and forgot to ask Coralia about it as quickly as it came to her, and she didn't think about it again.

As Claire glanced around, she noticed that there wasn't exactly a dedicated path, which she found quite unsafe since she assumed that there were submarines driving around, for she saw some parked during her earlier rush to Cora's home.

While she was swimming alongside Coralia, she brushed up against one of those trees. It most definitely should have left her with a scratch, but when she peered down at her arm, she saw nothing. *Odd*.

"There it is," Coralia said.

Claire was ripped from her thought.

From meters away, the market glistened. Claire had turned her head for half a second and then the market was suddenly there when she turned back. Claire found the pattern on the ginormous, shiny turtle shell to be so beautiful in the way that it was like a decoration on the protective shield of such a lovely creature. It was, in fact, much larger than the average house. Claire's eyes widened. She had never ever heard of a turtle that giant. She stopped dead in her tracks.

"Was there a turtle that was actually that big?" Her mouth gaped.

Coralia laughed slightly before she turned around. "Oh no, dear. We use magic to enlarge and alter the appearance of the things that we find in the sea."

*Phew*. Claire didn't know what she would do if she found a live one of those down there in the water. Probably get eaten by it in one bite. Claire just nodded, still awestruck by what she was approaching.

*So that's how Cora's bottle home is insanely giant. They can enlarge the things they find.*

A few submarines were tied to the giant shell and anchored down around the structure. As they got to the very front of the market, Claire noticed that their shopping carts were quite interesting. They were live sea turtles, snapping their jaws at her. Instead of their shell being normal, like a hump on their back, it caved in like a bowl. Claire moved away quickly while Coralia moved closer to them, doing the same thing as the night before on their way to Claire's suite. She closed her eyes, looking as though she was summoning something. Then the turtle in the front of the line turned and proceeded to head her way like it was a robot. Claire simply watched in amusement. Those turtles were one of the strangest animals she had ever seen. *Are they all like that, under some spell to do as they are commanded? Boy are the merfolk powerful.* And to think about all the things that they could simply do with just their mind. It was terrifying.

As soon as they swam in, two employees were there to greet them.

"Luke, Holden," Cora said. She nodded and glanced from one to the other.

*Oh great*, Luke was the one that saw Claire in her panties. Her heartbeat picked up again. And goodness, he made her stare in awe.

"I'd like you to meet Claire; there's a possibility that she may soon be a new resident here, so you may be see—"

"Oh, I don't know about that. I—" Claire's voice broke off; she didn't know what else to say.

They both shook Claire's hand, hooking thumbs.

"Pleased to meet you," they both said politely.

Luke locked eyes with Claire, acting as though he had never even seen her. Did he not remember? Did he not know it was her? Maybe that was for her own good. She still felt her cheeks flush, though. She didn't exactly know how to act.

"You as well!" she said. "Both of you," she added with a shy smile.

Holden, who was almost as tall as Cora's husband, had eyes the color of oak and dirty blonde hair that swayed in the crystal-clear water. He had to be no more than twenty-five and was quiet in a polite way.

Luke, on the other hand, was slightly shorter, tattoos galore, jet-black hair, and eyes the color of the ocean. Claire hadn't seen the combination of blue eyes and black hair before, but she liked it; it was unique. *Alluring.* Luke looked a bit older than Holden, his face more mature, maybe around the age of thirty. As the four of them conversed for a few minutes, Claire studied Luke. He seemed to be the more outgoing one, holding eye contact well and knowing the perfect time to ask meaningful questions.

"See you later!" Claire exclaimed.

They both nodded. "You will!" Luke called back.

Wow, it was quite chaotic in there. It was dark, resembling an igloo, with only a few skylights placed around here and there. The water was almost *thick.* It was very different from what Claire envisioned it would be after seeing the pretty and bright exterior. It was rather bleak. However, while it was quite dreary, it was also a moderately stocked market with an extensive selection of peculiar food. Claire could hardly choose just one thing for her eyes to land on—the butcher slicing up fish and other sea life with his sword, their produce section that looked like plants simply growing out of the ground, or the wooden sign that said *Barnacles? Oh no. Ew. Do they eat barnacles?* Claire grimaced. She would find out soon enough.

From a quick glance, Claire saw makeshift glass cabinets crafted out of sliding glass doors and windows and anything glass that the mers must have salvaged from the sea. They held Zubbles and various sizes and shapes of jars and potion-like-looking bottles. There were various foods and liquids inside of them, depending on where in the store you were.

As Claire swam next to Coralia in the store, keeping a close eye on the snapping turtle cart, she thought about how crazy it was that she was able to breathe, hear her surroundings, and smell, all underwater. She couldn't completely wrap her head around it. It was the most bizarre thing, as if she wasn't underwater at all. There was no pressure on her lungs, and the water didn't burn her eyes as it normally would.

*Did I die?*

The thought still haunted her. But there were too many distractions now, so the thought couldn't linger for too long.

She looked down for the first time, noticing that the floor was sand like most of the other places she had been. Then Claire noticed that Cora was making her way to the barnacle area. *Great.* A giant, scrap-wood sign with various types of handwriting etched into it and what looked to be prices, hung above the barnacle business area.

"Hello!" Cora called out cheerfully as she approached the area.

The merman gave her a smile and nod, not seeming to find it strange that Claire was there. "What can I getcha?" he asked. His voice was raspy. He didn't exactly look too old, but some of his features said differently.

"One tail of a month old, please!"

*Tail? If it is exactly what it sounds like, ew!*

Had Claire eaten that the other night in her dinner? She didn't even want to think about the fact.

The man nodded to Coralia, pulling a piece of rough barnacle from under the old, worn, wooden counter. The counter looked as if it had been a desk at one time. He lined up his sword perfectly at the one-tail marker on the counter and chopped down hard, little bits of barnacle floating away as he picked up the large piece and offered it to Coralia. Their tail measurement was about equal to a yardstick. She politely smiled at him as she took it, then opened the clear dome on the turtle cart's back and slipped it in.

"Thank you!"

*Oh boy, where to next?*

The turtle turned down the closest aisle. Cora hadn't even commanded it. *Can it read her mind?* That was a scary thought.

Long planks of wood and scrap metal created shelves that were packed full of jars and bottles. Claire floated along, admiring them all. So many colors. Then she saw one that said *Eye Spred.* She grimaced, quickly snatching it up. *Ew, ew, ew.* She examined the gloomy, grey concoction. She didn't *see* any eyes. "Cora, what—what is this made out of?" She looked quite disgusted. She wasn't so sure that she even wanted to know.

"Eyes. Sea creature eyes. It's sort of salty."

*Is it actually made of eyes? Gross.* She set it back down. *Coralia has tried it? Yuck.*

There were a few very oddly named things on the shelves, but most seemed fairly normal *for the merfolk world.*

Behind Claire, Coralia placed a few things in the turtle cart. Claire had already seen one of the items on the shelf—*Corals Spred.* Not terribly strange. But the blue, glowing, potion-looking bottle that Coralia picked up was quite alluring.

Claire often found herself feeling as if she was being watched inside the market. She felt like everywhere they went, the same worker was there, watching her or swimming past them. However, the mer's dark reddish-brown hair was always flowing just perfectly to cover her face whenever Claire would turn to look at her. But Claire tried to suppress the uncomfortable feeling that the mer gave her and kept a close eye on her surroundings. Besides, she was a new human in a world of merfolk.

After the *Eye Spred* encounter, they were off to the produce section of the store. It was like a corn maze. Some of the plants stretched high over Claire's head, and some were thick and covered the ground. Most of the produce was not known to her, each of them having their own bright, distinct color. She ran her hand over one piece of fruit that looked as smooth as glass, but she quickly pulled her hand back when she felt like it cut her. She turned her hand over expecting to see blood leaking from a scratch, but there was nothing.

From that same hidden pocket-like compartment in Coralia's tail that she had pulled the nail polish out of, she whipped out a tiny dagger; it sparkled in the skylight. She gripped it firmly and grabbed onto the plant that she was about to harvest, grabbing a huge chunk of it. The plant was lime green with tons and tons of little beads hanging off it. She sliced about a foot of it out of the middle and wrapped something around it that looked to be fishing line. Afterward, she threw it into the cart.

The turtle hadn't tried to snap at Claire again yet, but she didn't trust it. She stayed several feet away from it at all costs.

"So . . ." Claire's voice trailed off. "Who is that Hudson?" she questioned Cora in a very curious way.

Cora looked down at Claire with a funny expression, knowing why she was asking. "Well, he is one of our monitoring system employees. Sometimes he works outside of the office, that's why you saw him. You know, in human years, I believe you two would be close to the same age," Cora answered in a suspicious tone, eyeing Claire.

Claire tried to sound as if it didn't matter to her one bit. "Oh, I see," she replied while running her hand over an aqua fruit. It changed color like a mood ring when she touched it. She assumed it must have occurred because of her warmth. Her eyes widened. That would have really shocked her a few hours before, but she was prepared for practically anything now.

*Human years? What is his age in merfolk years?*
"Why do you ask?"

Cora's question caught Claire completely off guard. "Oh, um . . ." she paused, trying to come up with something believable. "Just making conversa-tion," Claire said plainly.

Cora gave Claire a nod, along with a strange glare. It was left at that.

Coralia peered around once more, the turtle halt-ing at the same time as her. "I think that is all."

*Well, that was a quick trip.*

They swam over to a small corner table, similar to the counter at the barnacle area, yet more of a wrap-around sort of counter. The cashier, a mer-maid, sat on a post behind it. Claire studied the young mer—studied the way she hadn't stopped smiling the entire time Claire had been watching her and studied how smooth her doll-like skin was. So as not to seem like she was staring at the cashier when they finally made eye contact, Claire turned her gaze to the mer's tail. Oh, how exquisite her periwinkle tail was! She seemed to have the perfect balance of beauty and kindness.

The cashier immediately locked eyes with the turtle, a red stream of light connecting them, as if they were mesmerized. Okay, now that was a little bit of a shock to Claire. A little freaky too. And then, nearly a split second later, everything went back to normal.

"That'll be five sand dollars." The young beauty smiled happily, bobbling back and forth. *The turtle just transferred the total into the cashier's mind.*

Claire wanted to laugh. *Sand dollars? Do they pay with sand dollars?*

From that same tail pocket that she pulled all the other items out of, Cora pulled out some sort of tokens that were in the shape of sand dollars. They all had different markings and amounts on them. She handed five of them to the cashier, and they were paid in full, free to be on their way to their next destination. As they floated out the door, they gave both Luke and Holden a polite smile.

"Have a nice rest of your day, ladies!" Holden exclaimed.

"Thank you! You two as well!" Cora replied as she glanced over at Claire. "Very polite young men they are!"

"Very much so," Claire added, blushing slightly as she passed Luke. She was thankful that things hadn't gone badly with that disturbing worker.

# Clove

Thoughts and curiosity flooded Clove's mind as she awoke once again to see Claire. She watched Claire carefully as the mer workers pulled the drowsy humans out of the jet. From what Clove could see but Claire could not, the workers took each of them to a room in the same building that Claire was staying in.

Clove could clearly see the worry and concern in Claire's eyes as she carefully watched her storm out of her room. Claire didn't even pay attention to the young merman gazing at her down the hall after bringing one of the humans in. He finally broke his gaze when she burst through the giant entrance doors. Claire looked to her right for a more in-depth view of what was happening. As she swam closer, the workers caught sight of her, but that didn't stop Claire. She kept on swimming. Clove watched as Claire and the workers conversed.

"I have a name!" Clove heard Claire shout angrily, as if she wasn't being acknowledged.

She saw that the worker watching Claire in the hallway joined the chaos. *She is not happy at all*, Clove thought. *Couldn't they see her suspicion? Obviously not.*

As Hudson lightly pulled Claire's arm, Clove could see the fiery glare in her eyes. She was sick and tired of people grabbing on to her, especially after what had just happened to her.

Even though Claire wasn't the happiest with those two mermen, Hudson was stuck in her head. She liked him, and no one could say otherwise. She didn't know if it was his smirk or how his luscious, dark hair flowed when he moved. Or was it his personality? *No, it certainly wasn't his personality.* Not yet anyway.

Finally, Clove watched Claire as she hurried to Cora's home. She knocked harshly on the solid door, ensuring she would be heard.

"Claire?"

Then Clove returned to waking reality.

Clove glanced around her room, remembering it was the middle of the night. She knew there wasn't anything she could do about the flashback now. Therefore, she lay back down, yawning. Clove shook her head. Gosh, she had Hudson stuck in her mind as well. *He really is dreamy*, Clove thought, then drifted back to sleep.

After several hours, she was awoken early that morning by their pit bull, Rosie, barking dramatically at a lizard that had gotten into their house. The silly dog was tough but at the same time would jump if she saw a fly. Clove laughed while lazily walking down the stairs, yawning and running her hand along the smooth railing, steadying her half-awake self.

"Real guard dog, huh?" Clove chuckled while petting Rosie, thinking about the flashback. Or was it? Had she simply dreamed all of it? Ugh. She was stumped and hungry.

As she made her way to the front of the house, near the family room, she heard a ball smashing hard against the ground.

*Roman.*

This time though, it was Roman and only Roman playing basketball. There was no sign of Lucas, and she was not at all surprised. She wasn't in the mood to go out and watch him. *Not today.* She wasn't very happy with him. He really needed to acknowledge that.

Crepes sounded like a nice treat, so Clove decided to surprise her family with breakfast. She found a boxed mix shoved to the back of her pantry that looked simple enough. She added water and eggs to it and started cooking them. While they bubbled and sizzled in the pan, she washed and cut some apples, strawberries, and bananas. Clove realized she had some extra time, so she quickly whipped up a giant pineapple smoothie and scrambled eggs to accompany their breakfast. All of that was easy and quick enough to do.

Unexpectedly, her parents came down the stairs just as she finished cooking the crepes, and her mother's mouth gaped open.

"Awe, sweetie, this is so sweet!" her mother exclaimed happily.

On the other hand, her father was still half asleep and not a morning person, so he just smiled. But Clove could tell in his eyes that he was grateful and proud.

"Roman, breakfast is made," their father shouted out the front door into the quiet street.

"I'm not that hungry," she heard her brother shout back.

He was old enough to know when to eat, so their father simply shut the door. Better for Clove's sake anyway.

The comforting aroma of sweet, melted butter filled their home. Although the crepes were slightly thicker than they should have been, they were still to die for. Clove indulged in a strawberry crepe and an apple crepe, both topped with a generous dollop of whipped cream. Her mother enjoyed two apple crepes, and her father ate enough for both him and Roman.

As they finished their breakfast, Roman was still outside playing basketball. He would do anything to not have to be anywhere near his sister. But she didn't mind. She didn't want to be continuously yelled at by him.

For making breakfast, even though she wasn't told to, her parents cleaned up and offered for her to do something she wanted to do with her time. Gardening was her choice, so Clove went and changed into some jean shorts and an old, cropped tank top, clothes she didn't mind getting stained since they already were. She grabbed her headphones, threw some gardening gloves on, and started weeding her succulents. Clove had not always enjoyed gardening, but she started to find it calming as she got older. She had sort of an old soul for her age.

Clove was jamming out to her music, doing much more dancing than gardening, enjoying her own company, until a small frog leaped out from a watering tube onto her and practically made her jump out of her skin. She gasped very loudly, swatted everywhere her arms could reach, then finally got it off and scared it away, grimacing as she walked since she could still feel its slime. She returned to the weeding, hopeful there weren't any more, but she knew there always were. Clove just wasn't a big fan of amphibians in general. It had been a long time since she had liked them even a little bit. Finding a giant frog in her toilet when she was little traumatized her. All she had wanted to do was quietly use the bathroom in the middle of the night, not wake her whole family up with her blood-curdling screams when she lifted the lid on the toilet to see the frog's beady eyes staring at her like it wanted to eat her.

Shortly after returning to tending to the garden, she found a ladybug. She counted its spots. *Eight.*

*Does that mean it's eight years old?* It flew away after Clove admired it for only a moment.

She was getting all sorts of surprises that day.

Clove heard a door shut loudly, and she popped her head up, craning her neck, quickly scanning her surroundings, finding that it wasn't anyone from her house. It was Lucas. *Good thing it wasn't Roman.* Lucas looked as if he were about to go for a swim. Before jumping into his pool, he peered her way and waved, and she waved back, a frown forming on her face. Then he dove in.

Ugh, Clove would not feel guilty for Roman's stupid behavior.

She didn't hear a ball dribbling anymore and assumed that Roman had finally gone in from his practice. Clove was satisfied with the outcome of weeding the garden and was getting hot from the summer rays hitting her. Beads of sweat were running down her face, but at least she had a glowing tan (as much of a glowing tan as her pale skin could obtain) and a weeded garden. She decided it was about time to turn in and started heading toward her house, away from the serenity of her garden.

Clove entered through the back door and saw no sign of anyone. In fact, she thought the house was a little too quiet. As she looked around, she saw that the TV was turned off and that the kitchen was completely spotless. Moving toward the front of the house, she caught sight of her parents hanging out on the swing on the front of their wrap-around porch. Stopping momentarily to admire them, she let out a breath, a soft smile settling on her face. That smile quickly faded though, when Clove thought about the fact that since Roman didn't appear to be downstairs, she would most likely find him upstairs, right where she was headed. After taking a deep breath, she quietly climbed the stairs, hoping they wouldn't creak. She didn't want to deal with him right then at that moment. Unluckily for her, she had to pass his room to get to hers. She attempted to walk past his room while tiptoeing, holding her breath, and not turning her head. He was putting a shirt on a hanger as she passed but turned just in time to get a glimpse of her, his expression growing hopeful.

"Clove!" he called out.

She practically flew into her room, slamming the door behind her. She heard his footsteps close behind.

"I swear, I'll stay out of your personal business, I promise, just . . ." He paused. "I really need to talk to you," he begged.

Clove thought for a moment, growing more annoyed with every word he spoke.

"Please, Clove," he added, just as she thought he wasn't there anymore.

With her face flushing and her throat tightening, she ripped her door open. She let out a huffy breath. "Fine," she snapped. Clove pointed at him like a disappointed mother. "And I'm going to hold you to your promise."

He slowly entered her room, walking past her and sitting on her unmade bed. "I'm sorry, I really am. If you knew the whole story, you'd understand better."

Her heart started to race, and she threw her hands up into the air, immediately regretting opening her door. Clove was so over the secret keeping. "Then tell me! Tell me the whole story!" she yelled, cutting him off.

"I can't . . . yet," he replied. He stared at the floor, fiddling with his hands.

"Well then, when can you? Because I'd really like to know what's going on! I'm tired of being the clueless one here!" Clove shouted out, suspicion growing as they spoke.

"It's more of something that Lucas should tell you, honestly."

She shook her head and then stared intensely at Roman. Clove didn't want to argue about it. She knew the truth would come out one day. *Has he really done something so severe? Has he maybe gone to juvie?* **No way.** Clove needed to change her mindset. She knew he wasn't that kind of person at all. In fact, he was quite the opposite. *Maybe it is just something extremely embarrassing to him? Was Roman involved?*

Ugh, her thoughts were going to consume her life.

"Is that all? Just coming in here to inform me that you can't tell me something?"

He gave her a stupid glare. "Actually, no." Roman stopped, cracking his neck, hesitating. "Why are you all of a sudden hanging out with him?" he finally asked, in a calmer, curious tone.

"If I told you, you'd think I'm lying or crazy. Or both. Trust me, it's not completely why you assume we're hanging out."

He nodded, looking dazed.

But it was the reason, sort of. Clove really couldn't think of anyone better to turn to with her curiosity than Lucas. She trusted him. And she also *obviously* wanted to hang out with him more.

"I seriously am sorry about how I went off like that the other night and how I've been treating you lately," he said. "Hang out with him or us if you want, in our house or his, whatever. I'm glad you two get along, and I'm sorry if I ruined it for you both."

"You didn't," she snapped back. "And I appreciate that, but I'm not the only person that you really need to apologize to." Clove eyed him, hinting that he seriously needed to apologize to Lucas.

He slowly nodded in agreement. "I can't go over there right now, not after treating him like that. I just can't. Where would I even start? What would I say? Sorry is not going to cut it."

"You're going to have to figure that out yourself!" Clove replied with a giant grin, as her phone made a strange noise, a noise that notifications and texts normally didn't. She glanced at it, realizing that it was from Lucas. That was why it sounded different. Clove hadn't programmed a notification sound for him yet.

> Hey, what's up?! Have you talked to your brother yet?

She read it as Roman gave her a questionable look.

"D—dang spammers!" She tried her best to sound believable while shaking her head and rolling her eyes. Still, her brother squinted his eyes at her, not completely buying it.

Clove quickly changed the subject. "Well, I need to shower, and let's not have the same thing happen that did the other day, so it would be helpful if you weren't in here." She motioned for Roman to turn around and leave.

"Oh yeah, sure thing." He quickly got up from the bed. "Just . . ." He paused for a moment. "Know that I really am sorry," he said, turning around quickly.

She nodded, not believing him and not really caring, then shut the door.

Why the sudden change of heart? Wasn't he just angry at her that morning? Was he attempting to lower her suspicion? Clove didn't want to think about it anymore. She didn't want to think about what the heck was happening to her or what was happening between her and Lucas. A peaceful shower was all Clove wanted. But she knew her thoughts wouldn't allow that.

As soon as Clove knew the coast was clear, she practically flew onto her bed, snatching her phone up and immediately replying to Lucas. After she finished, she didn't fully trust that Roman wouldn't come back into her room and read her texts, considering he looked suspicious of her earlier. She turned her phone off and stuck it in her secret wall safe behind her vintage mirror, a secret compartment her father constructed just for her when she was little to hide her "valuable" costume jewelry. Roman wouldn't even think to check there. *That'll buy me some time*, she thought.

Clove stood in her bathroom for a moment after her shower, simply enjoying the sugary aroma of one of her favorite skincare sets, *Twistee Twirl.* Then she remembered she needed to check her phone and rushed back into her room. It was turning on slowly, though. "C'mon, c'mon!" she urged, pacing back and forth.

As soon as it got a signal, a text popped up from Lucas. Lucas said that Roman saying sorry would be just fine. She thought Lucas was being a little too forgiving.

She wanted to know so badly what they were hiding from her, so she just asked him. *The worst outcome is that he will say nothing at all.*

Only a few minutes passed by before Lucas replied, but those minutes felt like hours to anxious Clove.

Clove walked into her bathroom right as her phone went off, and she just about fell over her own feet while hurrying to get to it. Her heart started pounding even though she knew that he wasn't going to give her an answer. And she was right, because he didn't. Lucas simply left her hanging, telling her that there was something that he should tell her, though, when she was older.

What kind of answer was that? To Clove, it was certainly a dumb one, an excuse to keep her away from the truth for a little longer. She exhaled deeply.

No problem. I understand.

She hit the send button, still curious as ever and disappointed. Some things were . . . very worth waiting for. And that was exactly what she would have to do, wait. And wait and wait and wait.

She finished getting dressed while running through her thoughts, trying to dream up some sort of reasonable explanation for everything, especially her flashbacks. She knew she couldn't exactly look into Lucas's secret keeping, but she could investigate the mermaid/flashback situation, so she decided to do some research for herself.

*Have mermaids been proven to be real?* She typed into the search engine on her laptop, feeling like a young child again searching for that. Finally, one of the top stories caught her eye: *Fisherman Says That Sonar Scans May Have Detected Mermaids.*

When she continued reading, there wasn't much information, and there was nothing proven, other than the man saying that he thought that it was a mermaid. Interesting but not very helpful to her.

After what felt like an hour of surfing the Web, Clove found a website that she had never heard of before: *The Realms in the World.* She eagerly clicked on it. She had a good feeling about that one. *Fairies, gnomes, elves, merfolk!* "Ah, yes!" she whispered to herself. Just what she had been looking for.

It took a lifetime to load, which wasn't helpful for her eager self. She clicked on it several times to try to get it to load faster; of course, it didn't. *When did that ever work in the past?*

At last, a page popped up.

She sat on her bed until her eyes felt droopy from all the reading. She couldn't believe what she read. So, merfolk would normally kill humans! And they *may* save you, but they'll just then kill you in the long run. All she could think of were the flashbacks to come. Is Claire going to get *killed?* If only Clove could warn her.

A knock sounded on her door, and she practically jumped out of her skin, gasping, her heart jumping to a race. "Dinner is ready," Roman called out.

Clove hadn't realized it was already that late, though her stomach was getting gurgly. She hopped off her bed and hurried to the stairs, meeting her brother right at the top of the staircase, the smell of garlic flooding her nostrils. He was headed downstairs for dinner as well.

"Talk to Lucas yet?" she questioned, wondering if she should ask such a risky question.

He shook his head while turning the corner into the kitchen, and Clove shrugged her shoulders.

*Mermaids kill humans?* She couldn't get the horrible thought off her mind. She started to gaze off into the distance, but her mother cut her day-nightmare short, thank God.

"Tacos tonight!" Iris exclaimed as Clove saw them sitting on the table on the giant plate that her mother always used for taco night.

They were filled with some of her favorite foods: scrambled tofu, salsa, pepper jack cheese, crispy iceberg lettuce, and a giant dollop of sour cream on top.

As always, half of the filling in her taco slid out onto her plate as she took her first bite, but whether it was on the plate or in the taco shell, it still tasted and smelled amazing.

They all had a love for tacos. So did Lucas. Clove wished that he could have come over for dinner but at the same time didn't because of the awkward situation. She still felt extremely guilty even though it wasn't her fault.

She began to gaze off into the distance, seeing Claire again, *another* flashback.

Claire floated at the doorway of Coralia's home. Cora, somewhat confused, invited Claire in and after a moment, offered her a seat. Claire was quick to question her. "Why was there a plane out there?" she demanded, suspiciously eyeing Cora.

"Clove?" Iris said sternly, staring at her daughter with narrowed eyes and a tilted head, stopping the flashback short.

How long had she been staring intensely at the wall? The flashback had only been a few seconds, but she felt like she had been out for longer. "Sorry, what?"

"Are you okay?" her mother asked, searching Clove's eyes very seriously. "Is something wrong?"

"You know, I think that being out in the sun today really tired me out. I have a bit of a headache as well," Clove answered, hoping that she sounded somewhat convincing.

"It'll do that to you," her father said, glancing up for only a moment, quickly getting back to finishing his dinner.

Iris looked at her husband and sighed slightly, giving him a look that said *something could really be wrong.*

Clove could tell that her brother's eyes were on her. He was the most curious, but she didn't dare to even glance at him. Clove very much lied; she was hardly even tired, but she had to act the part even though it was barely six in the evening.

After cleaning up dinner, she went back up to her room, and not far behind her was her brother like a shadow. He peeked through her doorway while raising an eyebrow.

"Come in," she muttered, rolling her eyes. She glanced down at her laptop.

"What's really going on? I don't mean with Lucas; I mean with you. You've been weird lately. And—and what was that at dinner?" His arm shot out toward the hallway. "It was as if your brain was off in another world. And for too long."

*I'm the weird one? Funny.*

She hesitated to tell him what was really going on. He was sort of on the right track. Clove completely trusted him on certain subjects and always had, but for a moment she was undecided on whether to tell him.

"I've been having more of those really strange flashbacks. That's part of the reason I've been hanging out with Lucas. He believes in some of that sort of stuff, so I turned to him," she answered.

A concerned expression washed over her brother's face as he rested his chin in his hand, completely focused on Clove. "What kind of flashbacks? Like the other one that you told me about?" he questioned. He moved closer to her, pulling out her purple desk chair and taking a seat.

She explained them all to him, one by one.

"God, I—I don't even know what to say except that I'm really sorry. That's why you and Lucas are—" Roman's voice cut off as he stared down at his hands.

Clove took a deep breath. "It is, and I do understand your worry . . . somewhat," she answered, still longing to find out Lucas's secret.

"I really don't even know what to say to that; I mean, a mermaid! That—that's insane!" he whispered.

"I'm still so confused. I don't know what to think of all of this."

Roman's eyes quickly shot open. "I've got to text him."

"Who?" she nervously asked, then felt dumb after he answered.

"Lucas! God, I'm such a jerk," he answered while storming out of her room, shaking his head.

After that, no more questions were asked, which surprised her. She certainly didn't mind it, though. She sat there for a moment, thinking, then stared off into the distance, again being transported to a different world. *A different time.*

The flashback wasn't as clear that time. It was like an old movie on a projector screen. How it continued to cut in and out was very strange to her. Luckily, she was still able to hear Cora tell Claire about the potion that was injected into the plane. *That's why the people that the workers dragged out looked drunk.*

Clove didn't think that Claire should have believed much of the information that they were feeding her.

Claire and Cora talked for a while longer. Then once some of the mysteries had been explained, the time for the tour had finally come! Excitement was surging through Claire's veins. She couldn't wait! The merfolk world truly was something unimaginable. *Unpredictable.*

*It isn't still around, though, right?* Clove couldn't believe she was wondering that. *The merfolk world isn't real!*

Clove could see that the one female worker that gave Claire an unsettling feeling had a barracuda ring wrapped around her finger, baring its teeth, ready to feast. Clove scowled, knowing it was only a ring but also knowing why the mermaid wore it. When she had been scrolling the website earlier that day, she read a paragraph that informed her that the mers who wanted humans gone wore that particular ring. Yet again, she wished that she could warn Claire because all she saw were bad things to come.

Claire and Coralia continued to shop, but Claire didn't realize that the worker who had been eyeing her followed her through the entire store. Clove was now extremely concerned for Claire.

As they left the market, Claire was happy she didn't see the mysterious worker again. It made her feel much safer. Little did Claire know, she was not far away, watching through a two-way mirror.

As the flashback left Clove's mind, she shuddered, then jumped as a small gasp escaped her mouth when she found her brother standing in her bedroom doorway, leaning on her door frame, staring straight at her.

"What?" she asked, weirded out. "How long have you been standing there?" she added before he was able to even open his mouth to answer her first question.

"A few minutes," he answered.

"Well, that's not weird at all, now, is it?"

"Did you just have one of those . . . things?" he asked her, seeming very concerned, and she proceeded to nod. "You looked possessed," he told her.

"Oh, really?" She laughed.

"What happened this time?"

"I'll explain tomorrow. I need some time to let it sink in. I'm kind of tired anyway," Clove answered, but Roman just continued to stand there. Then the reason why he was still hanging around popped into Clove's mind. "Did he text you back yet?"

"He did, actually..." Roman paused. "He said that we're all good."

"I'm so glad to hear that!" Clove faked a smile from ear to ear, knowing they were not just *all good.*

# Claire

Once they swam out of the market and back into the less gloomful atmosphere, Claire and Coralia started on their adventure back to Coralia's home. Although right as they did, a giant stingray started a game of chicken with Claire. Coralia could see a worried expression wash over Claire's doll-like face.

"It shouldn't hurt you; just move way out of its path," Cora quickly shouted, and Claire immediately moved.

Within seconds, it swam past her as if it hadn't done anything to begin with.

"Want to do something fun?" asked Coralia curiously.

"I—I think so?" Claire answered slowly, in a sort of questioning tone, not completely positive about what she was agreeing to.

Then, out of nowhere, Cora took a sharp turn at the side of someone's house. After a moment of hesitation, so did Claire.

"Isn't this trespassing?" Briefly glancing into the house, Claire could see right through.

"No, no, this is a dedicated route to the Sand Way."

Claire didn't completely believe her. That was a silly place for a dedicated path. Behind the house was a sort of clearing, a long stretch of nothing but wildlife and nature, what Claire thought to be the aquatic version of a prairie. Several species of water plants and those odd stick trees grew all around. Up ahead of them, a ginormous, perfect circle of sea glass began to appear, shimmering and sparkling like diamonds, rubies, and emeralds.

"That is one of the hundreds of entrances to it."

Claire grew almost speechless. She searched for words. "That—that is—extraordinary!" She wasn't paying attention to anything around her and accidentally rubbed up against one of the strange, sharp plants, causing her to bleed. Had she seen it wrong, or did it just *bite* her?

"Oh, goodness!" Cora came to a harsh stop and swam up close to Claire's cut leg, getting a better look at it. She very quickly swam over to the plant that had scratched or bitten Claire and ripped parts of it off. *How is it not tearing her apart?* She cupped the pieces in her hands and became deeply focused on them, whispering something below her breath. Claire could only see her lips move. Claire could only hope that she wouldn't use whatever she was creating on her. Then she swam closer to Claire once more.

"You're not going to use that on me, c—correct?"

"It might hurt slightly."

"No, no, you can't do that. It's going to really hurt me." Claire started to turn away right as Coralia smashed it into her injured leg. "Ugh, that stings!" Claire cried out, almost mesmerized while watching her blood being carried away by the rapidly flowing water, realizing that the pain from her twisted ankles was gone as well. She had completely forgotten about it until just then.

"Oh, but it works!" Cora laughed, pointing to Claire's leg that now didn't have a single scratch on it, only the lightest of scars.

Claire's mouth gaped open, her eyes wide. "Thank you?"

"Would you like to take the tunnels the rest of the way to my home?" Cora questioned.

"I would!" Claire exclaimed, grinning down at the trap door that led to the mysterious tunnels that she was about to be in. Claire wasn't so sure she should follow her into some random tunnel, but then again, what would the merfolk do to her if she didn't? They were insanely powerful. The tunnel entrance appeared as a sewer pipe lid. It was camouflaged with seaweed that grew directly on top, swaying in the crystal-clear water. *Is it real?* Claire wondered, since most plants couldn't grow on metal. Coralia pulled on a giant handle that was crafted out of bent brass, and an entrance that most passers-by wouldn't notice appeared.

"Come on!" Cora excitedly motioned for Claire to follow her.

"Wow," Claire whispered to herself upon entering the tunnel, but she didn't have much time to simply float and observe, for the crowd was moving quickly. And so, she began pulling herself through the tunnel with the brass bars that were on either side. Mers swam in and out of doors leading to small shops tucked away in the sand, and submarines floated by her like cars on a highway, dropping merfolk off at their destinations. It reminded Claire of the hustle and bustle in her small town during Christmas time. *Is it always like this?* Claire wondered as they passed by what appeared to be a salon. *Do they even celebrate Christmas? They must;* Claire convinced herself. Or at least their own version of it. As she eagerly watched through the salon window, she saw one stylist styling many mermaids' hair with squiggly brushes and another one working on their nails, throwing all sorts of glowing balls at the women. *Spells? Couldn't they use their magic at home? Perhaps the salon is simply for the luxury and enjoyment?*

Even considering that they were in an echoey tunnel, Claire couldn't believe how noisy it was. As she looked up, she saw that there were more shops tucked away in the crown of the tunnel, further explaining the ruckus. *How far down in the sand are we?*

Next, she swam by what looked to be a plant shop. *Green Goddess Goods* was inked across a plaque above the entryway. A few flowers and plants unknown to Claire floated in the tiny window. The twinkling lights that were strung throughout the shop created an enchanting ambience. She peered across the tunnel, over the line of submarines and saw even *more* shops. *Clancy's Can-*

*dies*, *Jerold's Junk* (which Claire could clearly tell was a junk store from all the rusted objects peeking through the window), *Marrisa's Mounds*, and *Norma's Bijous*. The shiny trinkets floating around inside Norma's Bijous caught Claire's attention.

Claire gently nudged Cora.

"Yes?"

"Could we go over there to the jewel shop?" Claire asked. She pointed to the other side of the tunnel where Norma's Bijous was.

Cora gave her a nod, and Claire smiled giddily, swimming into the glass tube that ran across the tunnel, over the submarines, to reach the other side. Pulling herself along, using the smooth, brass railing, she couldn't get to the jewel shop quickly enough, and the crowd of mers and sea life was certainly not helping her anxiousness.

Finally, she found herself floating through the hobbit-hole of a doorway. The old scent inside reminded Claire of her favorite antique shop. Shells of all sizes were strung onto what looked to be a fishing line, framing the very top of the teeny shop. It was so neat to Claire to be able to see the different shades of sand through the glass walls of the shop. She admired each and every pretty little jewel that overflowed from old bottles and vases which sat inside of Zubbles.

She looked Coralia's way, her hand on the zipper of a Zubble. "May I?"

Coralia nodded.

Claire unzipped it and ran her finger across some of the jewels. It was so bizarre sticking her hand and arm into thin air when her body was still in the water. The whole contraption was mind-blowing. It felt like sticking her hand through a portal, water on one side, and not on the other. Some of the gems were smooth, and some were rough or spiky. Then she got to the last of all the huge stump display tables, that one towering up to her chest. Coralia trailed behind her looking around for additions for her tail. Hearing a light cough, Claire gasped and jerked backward. Once her heart calmed slightly, she dared a peek behind the stump, where she thought she had heard the noise come from. Two old, nearly translucent, blue eyes stared up at her. She gasped again.

"Hello," Claire said as her voice squeaked and cracked. The mer looked like one of the oldest you could find. Claire could only imagine how old she was. Her skin wrinkled dramatically as she smiled softly, and she had the hands of a hero—weathered and wrinkly. And she sure was teeny tiny. Four and a half feet at best. She looked happy to see a young face. She pulled herself up from her weird chair and scanned Claire from head to toe. *What is she about to do?*

The old mermaid laughed. "Well, you sure don't look like you need jewels!"

Claire pointed back toward Coralia. She didn't know what to do or what to say.

The mer watched Claire become flustered before saying, "I'm just joking around with you, sweetie." She stuck her small hand out toward Claire. She had a firm handshake.

Claire would never get used to their weird handshake.

"Norma. And you?" Her voice was weak.

Wow, it was Norma herself.

"Claire."

"Well, Claire, I haven't seen you around before."

"I was brought here just last night," Claire explained, being brought back to the horrific night before in her mind, shuddering, then imagining all that the elderly mer had been through in her lifetime.

Norma raised her eyebrows and nodded Cora's way. "She saved you, didn't she?"

Claire nodded. Cora must have been quite well-known around there.

"Well, Claire, you let me know if you need anything." She picked up a giant rock off a tattered book and picked the book up off the ground. The book began flipping through pages all by itself until it landed on one in the middle. That must have been where Norma left off. "I'll be here, reading this!" She held the book up proudly.

Claire gave her a polite smile. *How is the book not ruined by the water? More importantly, how is it flipping through pages by itself? And how old is Norma? Hundreds of years?* **Thousands?** Her hair was as white as white could be, but it was healthy and thick looking. Claire could only imagine her beauty in her younger days. By her current appearance, oh, how she must have glowed!

Claire stopped and looked around, staring at all the gems glimmering in the soft, golden light that was cast throughout the shop. Pinks, blues, yellows, greens. What would a tail with every single type of gem in the store on it look like? Either hideous or stunning. Claire could have stayed in there forever. It was so peaceful—*magical.*

But right then, Cora looked her way, her eyebrows raised. "We should get going," she said.

"Nice meeting you, Norma!" Claire remarked, peeking over the makeshift counter, smiling big.

"You too, young one. I hope to see you around."

And with that, they were out the door and back into the chaos. Claire had been so focused on all the dazzling storefronts and stunning mermaids that she hadn't been paying attention to what was in front of her the least bit.

"Watch out!" Cora yelled out to Claire, still behind her, but it turned out to be too late. Claire spun around just in time to hit a familiar figure and knock the giant mound of freshly harvested seaweed out of their arms. Claire's eyes widened, and she gasped while raising her hand to cover her mouth when she realized who it was. *Hudson.* All the seaweed went floating through the crowd, and her face started to turn a very noticeable shade of pink after seeing the mess she had caused while her head was up in the clouds.

"I am so sorry," she said slowly, after taking a moment to gather her words, her jaw still ajar.

A smile played on his lips, and he laughed.

*This can't be the first time that this has happened, right?* Claire could only hope.

"Oh, don't stress it!" he said, waving his hand. He seemed to be in a much friendlier mood than earlier. "Claire, right?"

She nodded, practically speechless again by the gorgeous fellow in front of her. "Oh, here, let me help you," she insisted, feeling like a complete klutz. She giggled slightly while grabbing the seaweed that floated through the water, almost out of her reach, and piled it back into the box under the netting that was holding it in until she came along. She sighed. "I am so sorry about that."

He shook his head. "It's alright. Honestly, don't worry about it." He seemed to be in a bit of a hurry.

"See you later?" she said as more of a hopeful question.

"I'm sure you will." Hudson winked as he swam away, pieces of the seaweed still floating around them like confetti.

Claire broke out in goosebumps and couldn't help but smile. *Did that actually just happen? And especially, to me?*

Cora floated up behind Claire after she peacefully watched the whole ordeal, amused, to say the least. As Claire turned around to see how many had been watching, still embarrassed, Coralia gave her a funny look, raising her eyebrows.

"I think he's fond of you, Claire," Coralia remarked. She raised her index finger to her chin, scratching it lightly, acting as if she was wracking her brain, clearly knowing that Claire was charmed by him.

Claire gave Coralia a surprised sideways stare. "Me?" she squealed in shock, then laughed. She could hardly believe what Cora was saying. "I—I highly doubt that. Boys don't normally acknowledge me at all. Besides, I seemed to be nothing more than an annoyance to him when he and I first met," Claire stated, unhopeful, yet still gazing around in amusement.

"Claire, I can't be for sure that he likes you, but I can assure you that he's like that with everyone at first, and he is never that friendly that quickly after meeting someone. *Never.* Pay attention to the little things," Cora remarked, taking a quick, sharp turn. Then she glanced back at Claire. "Because sometimes, they *are* the big things!"

Claire's thoughts were twirling in her mind as they swam off.

"Here is our exit."

"Oh!" Claire exclaimed, not wanting to leave so soon. After they entered the sparkling, glass tube—*the transporter*—Claire studied the gem buttons that had Roman numerals etched into them. She counted them; there were at least five levels hidden beneath the surface of the sand. Claire wondered if she would ever have the chance to explore them all. Coralia pressed the arrow pointing up, and they shot up like a rocket through the layers of sand, which faded into lighter shades as they moved closer to the top. It was only a matter of seconds before the doors slid open. The tube that they were in popped out of the ground. It was as if a portal opened in front of Coralia's home. Claire was confused.

"There are portals all throughout our world. I just happened to get extremely lucky that there happens to be one right here!" As they swam out, the transportation system disappeared behind them, sinking back into the sand.

After a short swim, they arrived at Coralia's front door. Cora focused strongly on her hand, drawing all her energy to it. *What is she doing?* Around her index finger, bright specks of light began to form and twirl in the water. They stopped within a split second. *Holy smokes!* Her nail grew into the shape of a key, strong and thick with precise edges. Claire watched closely as she slipped her nail key into the keyhole on the gold door handle, wiggling it around and unlocking it. Had it not been locked the other night? Or had Claire not seen her transform her nail? They went into the house, Claire keeping a close eye on Cora's nail as it began to shrivel back down like a rose petal that fell to the ground. Dry, shrinking. Claire's mouth was gaping.

Coralia looked over her way and smirked. "Pretty neat, huh?"

Claire nodded abruptly. *Pretty neat? No, that was incredible!*

"I'm home!" Cora announced after she floated through the door. She glanced behind herself again at Claire. "He must be at our store."

"What store?"

"Lou is the top tail designer and distributor here."

"Tail design? Now that, that sounds like a delightful job!"

"Oh, it is!" Cora smiled, nodding her head as if she was thinking back to a great memory. "You know what? We should swing by there on our way to the monitoring office!"

Claire's expression grew very bright. "Really?"

"I suppose so. Perhaps you could even put an order in for a tail so that if later on you decide that you want to live here, you'll at least have a tail!"

Claire nodded slightly. It was a huge, life-changing choice to make. So much had already impacted her in the last day that she had been there that it seemed like an offer almost too good to refuse. Claire knew it would be one of the hardest decisions that she would ever make in her life, but she felt that the risk was worth taking. *Sort of.* She would also be letting go of a lot too. "What exactly would I have to do to live down here?"

"First, obviously, you'll need a tail." Cora laughed, and Claire nodded, being polite but already assuming that. "The tail treatment will take anywhere from eight to twelve hours. But it's absolutely worth it!" Cora said enthusiastically.

To Claire, she sounded innocent and honest. Claire wanted to believe her completely and trust them, but she also didn't want to let her guard down too soon.

"After that, you could live with Lou and me for a while and wait to see if you meet anyone that you would like to share a home with, or you could get your own structure to call home. But first, we will have you sign a contract stating that . . ." Cora hesitated. "Stating that you agree to the consequences of speaking about our world. You must agree to letting us memory wipe you if you later decide to return to pursuing life on land."

"What—what *are* the consequences?" Claire asked in a low voice.

Cora quickly whipped around in the water. "I am not at liberty to discuss such matters at this time," she answered while they floated out of her home, heading to *Too Many Tails*, her and Lou's company.

Claire gulped. Would she ever be informed of the consequences? Or were they something one simply had to blindly *trust* and *agree to*? Despite the unknown consequences and all she'd be letting go of, that strong pull on her soul continued begging her to stay. *What does it mean?*

"Is the tail process . . ." Claire's voice trailed off. "Painful?" she finally asked.

"Oh, it certainly can be, but not horribly."

Pain didn't bother Claire much, but she had a feeling that it would be more painful than Cora led on.

"Do I have to create my own home?" Claire was very curious.

"Normally, mers wait to create a house until they are devoted to another, then they build one together. I'd advise that if you want your own home, rent for a while, then decide if you are going to build one by yourself. Truly get a feeling of what you like."

Claire nodded. "Would I rent a house like yours, or are there apartments like there are in the human world? And what about income?"

Cora smiled; she didn't even know where to start to answer Claire's questions, but she was happy that Claire was eager to learn. "There are slightly larger versions of the suite that you are staying in now, which have full kitchens and a larger sitting area. Those are very popular among the young mermen and mers in general who are taking their first dive into adulthood and for some that just don't have a family. For example, that's what Hudson lives in."

Claire zoned out for a moment at the mention of his name, daydreaming. She shook her head. "I'm sorry; what did you say?" Claire apologized at last when she zoned back in, and Cora gave her a funny look.

"Hudson rents one of those since he doesn't need anything huge, considering he doesn't have a family of his own . . . yet." She gave Claire a goofy smile, the kind that your best friend would give you when she found out that you liked a certain boy.

Claire shook her head and laughed. "Oh, please! *What* are you saying?" Claire shook it off—on the outside, anyway.

"The apartments are just the perfect size too. One costs around fifty dollars monthly to rent. And for income, someplace is always hiring, just like on land!"

Claire was deep in thought, wondering if she could provide for herself at such a young age. "I understand."

"Well, look at that, here we are!"

Claire had been so preoccupied, thinking long and hard about her near future, that she hadn't noticed the gigantic neon sign that towered in front of her. "Wow!" she exclaimed, gawking at the fancy letters that spelled out *Too Many Tails*.

A giant castle came into view, and her focus shifted away from the very noticeable, bright, flashy sign. The castle looked as if it was ancient and so strongly built that not even a bulldozer could destroy it. "That castle is your store?" Claire was astonished.

"Indeed it is!" Cora answered while Claire floated beside her.

"How?" asked Claire, out of breath, scanning the area.

"It was all here. We were able to salvage and restore almost everything."

*The castle, the sign, everything. Wow.* It was like they had simply taken a castle and stuck it underwater; everything was so perfect, from the three flags swaying in the water to the giant sliding gate leading into the castle. Two guards, dressed in thick armor with giant, sharp tridents in their grips, floated at the gate and nodded to the ladies, every part of their body covered in heavy metal.

"Cora, when was this built?"

"The medieval times," she said, looking as though she was deep in thought. "Somehow, all of this water must not have been here!" she finished, a small laugh escaping her mouth as they entered the oldest, historic landmark that Claire had ever been in.

Claire's eyes widened as she peered up toward the ceiling to see a twinkling chandelier that she didn't even want to imagine the price of. Her delicate jaw dropped as she swam into the castle, thinking that if she were walking around with socks on she would most likely slip on the pristine, sparkling floor of the great hall. She spun around in a circle admiring all the tails that filled the walls from the floor to the towering ceiling. She could barely see the wall at all through all the rows of tails. Some were simple, and some were over-the-top, smothered in jewels, glistening in the soft light. "Wow!" she whispered, not able to find just one for her eyes to land on. They were all too stunning and eye-catching. "You two are so extremely lucky to own such an extravagant piece of history!"

"Oh, how we are!" Lou answered for both him and Cora. Not realizing he was there, Claire was slightly spooked. He hugged Cora from the side, and planted a soft, quick kiss on her lips.

Claire slowly gazed around, amazed at all the magnificent tails. "H—how much does a tail cost?" Claire knew that they had to cost a fortune.

"They range anywhere from one hundred to one thousand! That, however, is in our currency, not yours. It depends on the factors that go into making one, such as the size, color or colors, if you want gems or not, and the powers that each tail possesses," Lou informed after glancing at Coralia to see who was going to answer Claire's question.

Claire thought for a moment. "How much does the average mer spend on a tail?"

"Great question!" Lou exclaimed. "You see, normally when someone first purchases one, they go for one of the much cheaper tails, trying to save their money, but the cheap tails don't last as long and are mainly to be worn for special occasions, not everyday wear. Therefore, yes, they may have just bought a tail for a hundred dollars, but if they plan to wear it every day, it's likely only going to last between one and two years." He stopped and took a quick glance around. "Why don't you come into my office, and we can discuss this more in-depth. Darling, would you mind supervising for a while?"

"Not at all!" Coralia cheerfully smiled. Then she made her way over to a worker that was writing something down on their arm with what looked like a long, pointed shell. A plain shell, the words disappearing seconds after they scribbled them onto their arm.

*Interesting. How does it work?* Claire was still gazing behind herself, curious, when Lou pulled open the heavy, cage door to his office. It was like a door to a chamber. She quickly snapped her head forward when he started talking and was intrigued by the room's appearance. The polished maroon floor sparkled in the bit of light that shone through the line of barred windows that met the ceiling, poisonous flowers (to humans at least) hung from the ceiling, books stacked intricately on indestructible, mahogany bookshelves covered any sign of a wall, and an L–shaped desk stretched across the far-left side of the office with a very fancy throne behind it. The atmosphere in there felt *mysterious—secretive*.

*Why must they hang flowers from every ceiling?* And if she didn't know better, she would have asked how everything wasn't ruined by the water, but she knew the merfolk's power. *Their strength. Their magic.* A small, old loveseat with fabric the color of Dijon mustard sat close to the entrance of the office, and Lou quickly made a gesture for Claire to seat herself.

"Ah, yes, thank you!" She let a breath out.

A single book sat on Lou's desk accompanied by some fragile feather pens displayed in a crystal-clear jar, as well as an oil lamp crafted from glass, and a small picture frame that was facing Lou. He smiled when he looked at it, a spark igniting in his eye. Perhaps it was a picture of Coralia or their children? *Do they have children?* Claire wondered how all the items on the desk weren't freely floating throughout the room.

After Lou explained the differences between the various tails, he said, "You know what, Claire, I've got a few extra minutes. Would you like to design a tail for yourself? In case, well, in case you decide to live here?"

An eager expression washed over Claire's face, and excitement coursed through her body. She gasped. "Really?" she asked, eyes wide and jaw ajar.

"Sure thing!" Lou exclaimed as he swam over to a hidden door that Claire thought was just the fancy, paneled wall. Through the doorway sat the core of his business, the tail designer and printer. He proceeded to unchain it from the ground and pull it out of the hidden room so that Claire could see it.

She had never, ever seen anything like it, not even close. Her eyes lit up in surprise as she studied the many buttons labeled with Roman numerals. "That sure is a lot of buttons to memorize!"

"Good gods, yes, I know, it's absurd!" Lou answered dramatically while holding down the power button.

"Now, you designed this?" Claire asked, curious as ever, yet still patiently waiting, her hands tightly grasped together in her lap.

"Indeed, I did! It took me almost five years too. You see, designing a tail isn't something we can simply do by using our magic, per se, and so I took that as an opportunity to design this machine."

Claire smiled at him softly.

"Alright, now, what colors do you want your tail to be?"

Claire gazed off into the distance. "I'd absolutely love a lavender and teal tail."

He pressed a few buttons while sliding his fingers across the weird, little, glass screen that was on the front of the printer. "Any gems?" he added while eyeing Claire. He raised a finger to his chin.

"Do you have a pastel peach or coral?"

"I sure do!" Lou exclaimed after searching the screen for a moment.

Claire was getting anxious as ever to see it, if that was even a possibility before it was printed. Claire wondered if Norma was their gem supplier.

"For powers, we have invisibility, teleportation, power absorption, mind reading, extreme healing, and if you return to land for a mission or anything of the like, flying. There's also shape shifting, time traveling, and potion holding. Now, for the terribly difficult part, you can only pick three," Lou finished with a frown.

Claire tightened her jaw in frustration, and Lou chuckled slightly. Claire was in deep thought for a moment, then let out a sigh. "Perhaps I could wait on that and proceed to the next step?"

"Certainly. I know it's terribly difficult."

Upon deciding an appropriate length for Claire's would-be tail, Lou proceeded to work on the magical machine with an extremely serious, focused expression for several minutes, mumbling things to himself, before asking, "Would you like to take a glance?"

Claire giddily swam out of the oversized chair that she had been sitting in yet tried not to act like a child jumping out of bed on Christmas morning. She floated, speechless, but she still had more questions than Lou likely had answers for. She saw the tail, the tail that could be hers one day, the day that she was kind of hopeful would soon come. She gasped. It was even more flawless and stunning than she could have ever imagined. "I—I—it's lovely! It's even more perfect than it was in my imagination." Claire was beaming, gazing down at the screen which displayed the sample of the exquisitely de-signed tail. "How much will it cost? If I decide to stay and purchase it, that is."

"That will be determined when you choose your powers. But remember, you don't need one of these tails. If you were to convert to mer, you would un-dergo the treatment to grow your own tail like all mers are born with. This one here would simply be used as a swap out for when you want to change your powers or appearance."

She nodded, pondering what great powers she would choose . . . if she even decided to stay.

"There's no need for you to make all those de-cisions now though. I will keep your design in the system in case you decide to stay. I don't want to hold Cora up any longer, so I should get back to work, but thank you for stopping by."

"Perfect. Thank you so much for . . . everything! I absolutely love the design!" Claire thanked him with a giant smile as they left the *magical* office.

"So . . ." Claire's voice trailed off.

"Where to next?" Cora asked, already knowing what Claire's question was going to be.

"Yes, where to next?"

"Far away," Coralia answered mysteriously.

# Clove

C love woke to a funny-sounding notification on her phone. *Who's texting me this early?* She wondered but tried going back to sleep without looking at her phone. Then the noise of another notification sounded in her ear just as she was about to fall back asleep. *Lucas.*

> Hey could we talk in person? Today?

Clove smiled at the thought. *Absolutely!* she typed but deleted it.

No, Clove.

She settled on that. She didn't want to sound like she was crushing on him or at least not *completely* crushing. Rolling over in her bed, Clove made a second attempt to go back to sleep. But obviously, he replied.





As always, she was excited to get a chance to be around him. By that time, Clove was almost completely awake. She went directly into her brother's room to tell him nice and early that she was going to Lucas's, so he could get any potential fit out of his system early.

As she entered his room, she noticed he wasn't there, but his phone was. *Weird.* A gust from the fan sent an open book's pages flapping, startling her. Then there was another ding, giving her a jump scare. This time, it *wasn't* her phone.

Yes, sure, it wasn't Clove's business to read her brother's texts, but she couldn't help herself. And she knew that Roman would do the same, however she also knew that didn't make it right for her to read his. But she was going to do it anyway. She checked over her shoulder to make sure no one was watching, then proceeded to make her way over toward Roman's un-made bed where his phone lay. She wiped her finger on her shirt to make sure she had no oil or lotion residue, then eagerly pressed the home button. It flicked on with a flash.

A message from someone named Madelaine sat unopened on the lock screen. In fact, the name had a heart next to it. A *red* one. That wasn't just a friend.

*Oh my God.* Isn't Madelaine . . . *Lucas's* girlfriend's name?

Clove's heart jumped to a race. Why did she have to be so nosy sometimes? That certainly wasn't what she wanted to find. Really, she wasn't sure exactly what she was going to discover. She surely didn't ever imagine that it would be that.

She peered down at the message. *I really need to just break up with him already lol!* the message read.

Break up with Lucas? Clove's heart sank. Her own brother was dating his best friend's girlfriend. Sure, it was just an assumption, but there was no better explanation for that heart. Why else would he have a heart—a bright red heart next to his best friend's girlfriend's name? She grimaced. *Great. Just great.* And now she had to keep a secret and act all normal around several people. *Fantastic!* Ugh, she needed to stop being so nosy. But she also needed to find Roman. It was early, and it was bizarre for him not to be in there. It almost worried her, because she didn't even hear the sound of a fly downstairs. She nervously looked out of his bedroom window, then peered down at the basketball hoop, and there wasn't a single sign of him down there either. Clove's heart started to beat beyond her chest, and she tried to calm herself, taking a few—more than a few deep breaths—then rushed down the stairs, taking two at a time.

Not in the gym, kitchen, laundry room, TV room, garage, or any of the other rooms that Clove frantically rushed around searching. Why did he leave his phone in his bedroom if he went somewhere? Especially if he was pursuing a secret relationship with his best friend's girlfriend. Why would he risk someone seeing a text from her?

As she passed the giant glass door leading to her quiet backyard in the early morning, she caught a figure in the corner of her eye. She raced outside, charging him, her bare feet squishing in the dew-covered grass and the wind whipping against her features. *Be calm. Be cool. Act normal.* But when she got closer, she noticed what he was doing. He was planting some succulents that she had mentioned she liked last time they were at the store together.

"God, Ro, you had me scared to death!" she yelled as she ran toward him. Then she bent down to wrap him in a giant hug, despite her frustration with him.

"Why?" he asked. He shook his head, whipping his hair back and forth, then ran a dirty hand through it.

"I—I thought something had happened to you. You're almost never out of the house at this hour. More specifically, out of your bedroom," Clove stated, with a bit of bite in her tone. She swung her hand up into the air. She loved her brother dearly, and she couldn't be too mad at him; he was doing something so sweet, and even if he wouldn't have been, he was entitled to leave his bedroom at that hour. It just frightened her, that's all. She couldn't lose him. She'd throw her own body over his and take a bullet for him before she would let a single thing happen to him . . . even if he had been a jerk lately.

"I'm sorry for scaring you—"

"No, don't be. You did this, and it's—it's perfect! Thank you." With a soft smile on her face, Clove gestured around her garden that had a few new additions in it. The succulents were the exact ones she said she liked. Roman had said that the one plant looked like a bunch of toes.

"I really am sorry. I just—I got so full of myself and turned into some monster. And for how you treat me, you don't at all deserve it. So, I'm sorry." Roman looked at the ground more than her as he apologized, and Clove nodded.

*Another* apology. How could he just say all of that so easily while stabbing Lucas in the back?

"So, you honestly don't care if I hang out with Lucas?"

He let out a breath. "Clove, I can't lie. To an extent, whenever my little sister goes within ten feet of a guy or shows interest in one, I'm never really comfortable with that, but I've somewhat made peace with the idea. So, go ahead. He's a good guy." Her brother smiled, hoping that they were back to normal again.

Was he just saying that and surprising Clove with succulents to keep her quiet about his new little girlfriend in case she found out about her?

"Well, thank you . . . for all of this!" Clove said while nervously looking throughout her garden, not totally buying his kindness. "Now that we are discussing it, I'm um—I'm going over to Lucas's for lunch," Clove announced in a high-pitched tone, then speed-walked away.

"Have fun!" He thought for a moment. "*Clocas*," he offered a couple name for them. He started laughing, finding himself hysterical.

"Thanks, Ro-boat!" She turned back just in time to see his blank stare as he shook his head. She said it because she knew that he didn't like that nickname. She knew that from now on, whenever she and Lucas hung out, they would be referred to as *Clocas*. Secretly, she didn't hate it, but she certainly wasn't going to let Roman know that. As she headed back up to the dark, silent house, she heard her brother let out a small chuckle.

Clove's parents were still sleeping at the early hour, so Clove only made breakfast for herself and Roman.

"Good?" Clove asked him in between bites of omelet.

"Much better than when you were younger. Thank you!" He nodded his head proudly, nagging his sister and laughing, still feeling much guilt for the complete jerk he had been to his sister and best friend, neither the least bit deserving of it. Or at least he was attempting to act the part. Clove sensed that he wasn't being completely sincere.

"Hey!" she hissed. "I was learning!" she finished, lightly banging her fist on the table, laughing, knowing that Roman was teasing.

"I didn't need to be your test dummy, though!"

They both laughed hysterically.

While finishing up breakfast, Clove's mind wandered off. She knew for sure that there was still something that Lucas was hiding, and she was very determined to find out what the mysterious secret of his was. She had so many curious thoughts, and not one single answer, except for that she would be told when she was older. *Well, what does that mean? When I'm twenty?* She chuckled slightly and tried to cover it, acting as if it was just a cough.

"What?" Roman questioned.

"Oh, nothing!" She proudly took another giant bite of food.

To break the silence, Clove stupidly brought up the main thing that was on her mind. "You know, the last few times that I even said a word about Lucas's girlfriend, he got weird. So . . . what happened?" Clove thought back to the text.

Roman froze for a moment. "Um . . ." He stared at her, like a murderer being interrogated. "She's a nice girl, but she just got . . ." his voice trailed off again. "You know, busy with personal things. I'm actually not sure if they're broken up or not."

"Did he tell you what happened?" Right at that moment, Clove knew that she had gotten ahead of herself and asked too much, too soon, and sounded like she was completely in love with him.

"Why must you know, Clove?" her brother demanded. It was his turn to question now. His chance to get *out* of the spotlight.

"I just thought maybe something terrible had happened."

"Oh, come on, Clove. You know you like—no, apologies for my mistake. Much more than like him. We all know it."

"I honestly can assure you that's not the reason I'm hanging out with him, *Roman.*" *Or not the entire reason.* Clove completely left her brother's statement ignored while leaving the kitchen table to situate her dishes in the dishwasher.

"He already knows that you do, that's for sure."

Clove rolled her eyes as she walked out of the kitchen, flicking off the light. They hadn't broken up. From Roman's uncharacteristic behavior, Clove was sure that he was dating Lucas's girlfriend. What was the chance that it was a different Madelaine? *A pretty slim one.* Oh, the weight that she would have to carry on her shoulders. And awesome, she was going over to Lucas's house for lunch!

Later in the day, she headed over to his place.

"Oh, Clove! Lucas told me you were coming over. And . . ."

Clove already knew what Candy, Lucas's mother, was going to say. "No, you didn't!"

Candy nodded, and Clove squealed and danced around in excitement. She knew something special was coming her way for lunch.

"Come in, come in!" Candy gestured toward the kitchen that smelled of so many delicious dishes, and Clove smiled big. She got distracted for a moment, searching for Lucas.

"He will be down in a moment. You can go get him if you'd like!"

"Well, I—I don't want to bother him."

Candy gave her a peculiar look. "Trust me, you won't," she said blankly.

Clove started toward the stairs; not wanting to seem desperate was the majority of the reason why she hadn't wanted to go get him. But she also didn't want to be rude either. Therefore, she went on her way up the stairs. They seemed never-ending. She wanted to try to scare him. Clove quietly tiptoed up the stairs and glanced into the bathroom. The door was open, and it was dark. He wasn't in there, clearly. She practically floated into his room; little did she know that he was thinking the same exact thing. He knew she was there. She gave his room a quick glance, getting her eyes caught on his fake greenery that almost fooled her.

"BAH!" He sprung out from his pitch-black, walk-in closet as she peeked into it and gave her quite the jump scare.

She gasped and threw her hand to her heart. She should have known. "Goodness, Lucas!"

"Trying to frighten me, were you?" he asked her, and she made a funny, guilty face.

"Yes, yes I was!" she stated proudly while standing up as straight as possible, almost reaching his shoulder.

They both burst out in laughter.

"You guys, lunch is ready!" Candy called upstairs.

"We will be down in a minute."

Clove smiled at Lucas and started to walk out of his bedroom as Lucas asked, "When's your birthday again? I'm sorry; I can't remember."

"August seventeenth, why?"

"Just wanted to put it in my calendar once and for all!"

*Why is that important to him?*

They finally made their way downstairs to the delectable combination of freshly made pita bread with tzatziki, Greek salad, and sweet baked plantains, some of her absolute favorite foods.

Clove hurried into the kitchen and took a deep breath. "Ah, that smells amazing!" She grinned at all the food. The pita bread was perfectly golden, and she could smell the plantains' sweet, buttery aroma in the air.

"I haven't made this in ages." Candy thought for a moment. "The last time probably had to have been when you came over and ate with us," she added, giving Clove a sweet smile. Candy pulled her in for a quick hug.

They all gathered large servings of the delicious lunch onto their plates, and each took a seat around the corner nook dining table.

"So, Mom, guess who's going to be fourteen very soon!" was Lucas's conversation starter the moment they sat down.

"Oh gosh!" Clove said while she rolled her eyes and attempted to hold back a laugh, and Candy immediately made eye contact with Clove.

"No way! We've been friends with you and your family for that long?" she asked, very surprised. "That means it'll be almost ten years!"

Clove nodded. "Wild, huh?" Clove was quite surprised at the thought herself.

"Any special plans for this giant number?" Candy laughed as she took a bite of her pita that was drenched with tzatziki.

Clove just shrugged her shoulders. "You know, I've been thinking a lot about it, and I just can't make a decision."

"You'll figure it out; I'm sure of it!"

"I know I will; it's just getting close!" Clove sort of smiled through a grimace.

"Any more plantains?" Lucas's sweet mother asked as she stood from her seat, heading toward where the cinnamon and sugar plantains were.

"Yes!" Clove and Lucas yelled out at almost the exact same time.

"To die for!" Clove said dramatically, taking the first, savored bite of her second serving.

Both Candy and Lucas laughed.

"I guess that means that I haven't lost my touch?"

Clove shook her head. "Absolutely not!" She grinned, filling her face like a young child.

"I'm very glad that they are just as good as you remember."

"They are *really* good, Mom."

The conversation went on for several more minutes until the teens devoured all of their much-favored foods.

"Thank you so much for lunch, Candy!" Clove called out as they left the kitchen. She glanced over at Lucas, admiring him, and kind of smiled.

"So, what's new?" Lucas questioned while plopping down onto his desk chair.

"Uh, a heck of a lot!"

"Really?" he asked, looking surprised, or at least somewhat.

"What was the last thing I told you; do you remember?" Clove quirked her eyebrow.

"I think it might have been right after she had been pulled through that portal or whatever it was into the mermaid world."

"Merfolk. Merfolk world, Lucas," Clove corrected him, laughing.

"Sorry, merfolk world."

"In that case, a ton of information has come to me since then. I mean, like three or four flashbacks. They were long too."

Lucas let out a breath. "Wow, alright then. And it's only been a few days since I last saw you."

"I know. They are getting longer and longer each time. Or at least it sure seems like it."

Clove peered around Lucas's bedroom. "Uh . . . where to start?" She solemnly focused on her thoughts for a moment. "Well, right after she got dragged through the portal, she was in this community center place, I think. I remember that it was full of poisonous flowers, but only ones that were poisonous to humans. Claire was really scared. She felt as if the mermaids were going to turn on her and harm her at any second . . ." Clove continued telling Lucas all about her crazy flashbacks, making him gawk in awe.

"But Claire was roughly awoken by an abnormal noise. It even scared me when I first heard it in the flashback." She shuddered.

Lucas interrupted her as she started to speak again. "Now, I can't remember what you told me weeks ago. Is it as if you are there with them? Or as if you are peering down on them?" Lucas asked, raising an eyebrow out of habit.

"It just depends. But when it's like I'm right there with them, it's so much more realistic. It feels like if she got hurt I—I could help her." Clove stuttered out of sorrow.

"You know, I thought that the events that you told me about earlier were sort of crazy, but it just keeps on getting better and better, doesn't it?" Lucas said, smirking, after Clove told him about the mysterious jet, and she broke out in a laugh.

"I know!" She chuckled, glancing out of the window that Lucas sat in front of, mainly staring at Lucas when he wasn't paying attention. "The reason that the plane was there was because at a certain height above their dome world you are able to see in."

"You don't mean—" Lucas stopped mid-thought, but Clove already knew what he was thinking.

"Yup, whenever planes are reported to have disappeared, it's normally them. Oh, and Lucas, Claire met this guy, Hudson. She really likes him. He's around her age too. She thinks that he's just dreamy. I mean, he is and all, and I really think that they are going to be inseparable. I just have a feeling!"

The flashbacks were like Clove's own private romance and fantasy shows, except more real and terrifying.

"Really, and he's a mermaid?" Lucas crossed his arms and gave her an amused look.

"Merman, Lucas, merman."

"Right."

"And yes, he is."

For a while, Lucas focused intently on Clove as she talked nonstop about her flashbacks, but after some time, he took a quick glance at his phone. "Shoot, Clove, I'm sorry to cut you off, but I forgot, I have baseball tryouts tonight."

She started to get up, knowing it was getting to be close to dinner time now and that she was successful at not slipping up about reading her brother's text. Thank goodness she had sort of forgotten about it until then.

Lucas stuck his arm out in front of her. "Wait, do you want to come?" His facial expression said that he knew his offer was a bit strange, almost like he regretted blurting that out.

"Sure. That'd be fun!" Inside, Clove would *absolutely love* to. But she wasn't about to just confess her love right there on the spot.

"Really?" Lucas acted quite surprised.

"Of course, as long as I'm allowed to. What time?"

"Tryouts are at four, and it's three now, which means that we would have to leave in about thirty minutes," Lucas answered as he texted someone.

"Do you happen to know if my brother is going? He hasn't mentioned it to me."

Lucas looked up. "That's who I just texted, actually."

"Oh, okay." Clove knew for a fact Roman wouldn't be happy to see her at Lucas's tryouts.

Lucas's phone finally dinged. "He's going!"

"Oh wow, I'm surprised! He hasn't said a thing about it," Clove answered.

"Do you think that it's too soon for me to ask if I can catch a ride with him?" Lucas wasn't exactly one to hold grudges.

"Does it seem like things are okay with you two?"

Lucas nodded immediately.

*If only he knew the things she knew.*

"Then ask. I'd say the worst that he could say is no." Clove looked away for a moment and then back at him. "Then again . . . that's a promise I can't make." She laughed nervously.

"Have you ever been to one of these?" Lucas asked as he eyed Clove when he glanced up from his phone.

"A tryout, no. Baseball games, yes."

"Then you're certainly in for a show. You'll get to see some pretty crappy players," Lucas snickered.

"Well, your brother said sure," he answered in a sort of uneasy tone.

"Really?"

"Yeah . . . I'm kinda surprised myself."

"I'll ask him if I can come with you two. I don't want you to get screamed at . . . again." Clove continued walking out of the room to head downstairs to grab her phone so that she could ask her brother the risky question.

"No, no, let me. Please, Clove. I don't want you to get screamed at either. I'll just text him. Call your mom and see if you can go."

Clove sighed. "Are you sure?"

"Mm-hmm," he mumbled, nodding.

Clove dialed her mother's number as fast as her fingers could maneuver across the screen. "Hey, Mom, um . . . Lucas asked if I want to go and watch baseball tryouts. So, can I go . . . please?"

"Who's driving?" Iris asked sternly, right away.

Clove quickly cleared her throat before replying. "Roman. Roman is." Clove thought that perhaps she had lost signal with her mother. "Mom?"

"I'm sorry," her mother's voice was on the brink of laughter. "Do you actually believe that he's going to let you ride with them?"

Clove grimaced even though her mother couldn't see her. "I mean, sort of."

"Okay then, well, you can go . . . if he will let you, that is. I certainly can't make him," Iris answered, laughing now.

"Really? Thank you!"

"Oh, what time will you be home?"

"Lucas, what time should we be home?"

"Uh, six thirty, seven at the latest."

"Hear that?"

"Yes, sweetie, that's just fine!" she answered, ending the call as Lucas's phone dinged once more.

"Your brother said yes; there's even an exclamation point."

"Jeez, what's he planning on doing, offing us both, getting rid of the problem?"

Lucas laughed slightly. "I don't think he's gotten to the point of considering that . . . yet."

"I sure hope not," Clove offered.

"I'll be back in a second; I've got to change," Lucas said, smirking his typical Lucas Lynch smirk. He sped out of his room, grabbing his baseball uniform on his way to the bathroom.

A few short minutes later, he came out, pulling his shirt over his head and down his body, his etched-out abs disappearing behind it. *Ugh.* Clove had always thought he looked *so* good in the uniform. His uniforms and suits, *especially.* Clove grew all tingly inside.

"I think that I like the color of that one the most out of all of them," Clove managed to say.

"Eh, it's alright." He shrugged his shoulders then sat back down on his bed, next to Clove this time, pulling on his socks and lacing up his shoes.

*Oh, and he smells so good.*

*Okay, Clove, snap out of it.*

He looked up. "Ready to go?"

Clove nodded and smiled, beyond thrilled.

# Claire

After exiting the castle, Claire anxiously stopped dead in her tracks. "Do we happen to get to use a submarine?" she asked, eager to get to the next adventure.

"Yes, we should use the submarine. It will be a longer ride if we take the scenic route, but I don't mind," Cora informed, knowing from the spark in Claire's eyes that she desperately wanted to take the submarine through the scenic route. "You want to take the scenic way, don't you?"

Claire nodded profusely. "If that's okay with you, of course!" she exclaimed like a giddy child with a giant smile.

"Absolutely!"

She had extremely high expectations for the submarine because of how amazing everything had been so far. However, she didn't remember seeing one at Coralia's. *Where is it kept?* Claire wondered. Once they took the very short teleportation trip back to the house, Claire found herself following Cora through the towering archways that held all sorts of strange knickknacks, from sea creature skeletons and bones to weird-shaped bottles with odd, colorful liquid inside. A side of the house that she hadn't yet been in. Her house was always so quiet. Most of the rooms were hidden by a wall of glass with colorful bubbles in between rising to the top repeatedly. So, much of Cora's home was hidden from Claire. When they turned a corner, the wall was cold against Claire's hand and was smothered with even more swords and tridents.

She gasped quietly. *Wow, they sure do like their weapons.* She could see those better than the ones hidden away in the crevices of the arches. She thought that they were so shiny and beautiful yet so scary and powerful. Too pretty to be used. Then, through another solid ship door, she was back outside of Coralia's home. *Why couldn't we have just gone around the outside of the house?* Claire raised an eyebrow at the question in her mind.

Claire proceeded out the door, but Cora stayed back slightly, just before the doorway. As Claire peered out at her fish-filled surroundings, she heard a light click. Just then, the sand only feet in front of her began to shuffle around and shake, almost vibrating. Something long and silver poked out of the sand. *The submarine.* Claire watched in a gaze. It slowly floated up from its hiding place, the sand floating off it and then covering the ground again like nothing happened.

At last, she was swimming into the first submarine she had ever been inside of in her entire life. It reminded her of a tin can with windows. She giggled to herself at the thought. In the front, the driver's seat and the passenger seat were similar to a car. And oh, were there a whole bunch of levers and buttons. Too many, in Claire's opinion. Peering into the back, Claire saw two more seats. Behind those was a bunk bed. The beds were small, thin, and didn't look too comfortable at all, but Claire supposed they did their job. Claire was confused by the setup. *Do mers sleep in beds?* "Is this some type of house-submarine?" she asked, puzzled.

"Sort of!" Cora answered. "Lou and I have the biggest passion for traveling, so a few years ago, we invested in this." She gestured around. "It cuts the costs down by a very nice amount when traveling. You see, instead of renting a room—"

"Rent a room?" Claire burst out, interrupting Cora. "How big is the world down here? How *far* do you travel?" she asked.

"Oh, it is thousands and thousands of square miles!" Cora seemed to find Claire's question quite funny. She could only imagine what went on in Claire's mind.

Cora pulled forward, toward the huge clearing behind her home. Claire looked around. It looked like the same clearing as where the Sand Way entrance was. Then Claire spotted sea glass twinkling far in the distance. It *was* the same clearing. By how easily Coralia was maneuvering around, to Claire, it didn't look like it would be too difficult to learn how to drive a submarine, even though they had an abundance of buttons and levers.

"What does a regular submarine look like?" Claire asked.

"Very similar to this. There are two-seaters and four-seaters. And if you're lucky, you might even find a six or eight-seater. Simply remove the kitchen and bed and you'll have a normal submarine. Depending on your budget, they also sell glass top and glass bottom ones. They are spectacular for watching sea creatures, especially those that glow at night!"

Claire was blown away and giddy at just the very thought of one. "What's the point of having this if you can simply teleport anywhere you want?"

"There's one downside to teleporting. It takes a toll on our bodies. I don't mean when you want to teleport from your house to the market; I mean when you want to get from one side of our world to another."

Claire nodded.

"This trip is going to take a couple of hours, so it would be quite a strain on my body if we teleported the whole way," Cora informed as they drove toward the tunnel system entrance. Once they got close to the entrance, a giant opening in the ground appeared, like the one that the submarine rose from, close to where they had entered the tunnels earlier that day. Several other submarines appeared out of nowhere and quickly formed a line behind them.

"I thought that we were taking the scenic way?"

"We are; we just have to take this for a few minutes to get to the scenic route."

Claire had gotten very nervous for a moment, thinking Cora had forgotten their discussion earlier. *Or worse—she had wicked plans in order.* Though the tunnels were extraordinary, she was excited to see the merfolk countryside.

After waiting, a little light in the submarine signaled they were in the clear to enter the tunnel. Claire about had a heart attack when they practically dropped down in the middle of a line of traffic, though there was a perfect, large spot cleared for them. She could now see the preparation that had to happen so they could use the tunnels, which included both sides of traffic to halt. Then, out of nowhere, a submarine would drop down. She wondered why there wasn't just a spot to simply merge. It was the merfolk world, so there had to be a reason for the craziness. There always was. They had some interesting techniques for accomplishing tasks down in the underworld.

"How often is there a . . ." Claire paused, trying to think, raising a finger to her chin. "A drop-down point, I assume you would call it?"

Cora thought about Claire's question momentarily, with a focused expression on her face. "Converted to miles, perhaps approximately every three." Cora was not completely sure of her answer. "So, we should only be down here for about six miles," she added with a smile.

"The traffic must get miserable down here sometimes," Claire speculated.

"Yes, well, that's where our lower system of tunnels come in handy!" As she spoke, a smile played on her lips.

"There's more?" Claire half-laughed.

Coralia slowly nodded. "Oh yes!"

Claire was constantly thinking about the decision she would have to make: leave her family and create a new one or go back and lose the opportunity of a lifetime. Was it heartless and selfish of her if she stayed? Deep down, she knew the answer; she just didn't want to admit it to herself.

Claire must have dozed off because the next thing she knew, she was being shaken awake by Cora. She rubbed her eyes until they turned red and squinted from the instant brightness of her surroundings. But when she gazed out of the submarine's window, she saw where her life could be complete—the merfolk countryside. All her worries disappeared, even if it was just for a split second. Each way she looked, all she could see was what looked to be a never-ending, sandy pathway surrounded by the emptiness of the country. When she looked closely enough, the path moved due to all the tiny sea animals crawling in it. It was so much different than the city that they had just been in less than a couple hours before. The hustle and bustle was non-existent. This new place was not the merfolk's; it was a sanctuary for the marine animals. A kelp forest ran on for miles and miles, slowly swaying in the water, divine shades of green and yellow. A few houses peeked through the forest's landscape. She could very vividly imagine herself having a house of her own there, in the mystical forest, one day. A wish. A dream. It drew her in.

"Now, how far are we from the main city?"

"Which one?" Cora asked with a small chuckle.

"The one that your house is in."

"About an hour and a half."

Claire liked the sound of that, a quiet area far from the city, with plenty of space to do whatever her heart desired.

Coralia attempted to get the submarine running again, but it wouldn't start. "Oh, isn't that just lovely!" Coralia let out a sigh.

"It's out of fuel?" Claire tensed her jaw, frustrated, hoping that was all that was wrong.

"It most certainly is. Let's visit this house and see if they have any."

Claire nodded and swam out of the submarine. The house sat far out in the distance, though much closer than their next destination, which would have been too far to swim or teleport to.

"What exactly do you use for fuel down here anyway?"

"Pearls."

"Pearls, really?" she asked, taken aback.

"We do. That's part of why the pirates break in—to steal our pearls. They don't use them for fuel and feel we are stealing their profit."

"My goodness! That's scary!" Claire didn't like what she heard. She didn't like not knowing the extremes that the pirates would go to in order to get what they wanted. She imagined that they weren't civil. Something else for Claire to take into consideration before deciding whether she was going to stay there or not. She couldn't believe that she was even *considering* it.

They were getting closer to the house now. The two-story, brick home had a chimney that shot up from the side, which made Claire think that maybe it was there before all the water too. Simple white paint was chipping off the shutters and pillars, revealing the wood underneath. And a porch swing creaked as it swayed in the water. She peered around as they swam up the steps, taking in the canopies of wild and free seaweed that danced in the water. Claire thought the giant seaweed to be mystical yet haunting, like its long arm-looking fronds could grab ahold of her at any moment and consume her. Coralia's knock on the door drew Claire out of her dark thought.

"Hello?" A young mermaid, who looked no more than Claire's age, cracked the door open, confused. Claire wondered if her deep-purple eye color was natural. She didn't think purple eyes were possible.

"Good afternoon!" Coralia exclaimed politely. "You see, I ran out of fuel for my submarine, and we've still got a long way to our destination. I was just wondering if you could possibly sell us some pearls, if you even have any?"

The young mer smiled and nodded, her jet-black hair flowing like a cloud around her head. "Wait right there," she answered, closing the door as a smile grew across Coralia's face. No more than a minute later, she arrived at the door with a generous number of pearls inside of a Zubble. "Here, you don't even have to give me anything for them."

Claire and Coralia gawked in surprise.

"That's much more than I want to take from you. I can't take all of that."

"At least take half, I insist!"

"Oh, please let me give you money," Coralia begged, but the kind mer shook her head in disagreement as Cora sighed.

"Well, you don't know how much this means to me. I truly can't thank you enough!"

"I'm happy to be able to help!"

Coralia started to turn away, heading back to the submarine. "Thank you so, so much, really!"

The girl smiled and waved.

Claire stared at Cora, dumbfounded. "That was awfully nice of her!"

"I don't know why she would just give them away like that. They are very precious down here. We certainly don't have an endless supply of them."

They chatted as they made their way down the long pathway that led back to the submarine, as an archway of trees with thousands of yellow sea horses wrapped around their branches calmly swayed in the water above them. To Claire, the trees looked dead. Just their shell was left. *Were they what was glowing the other night in the distance? The seahorses?* Claire still wondered if she was just having a dream. It was all too surreal.

Once they arrived back at the submarine, Cora swam up to the top and poured the pearls into an opening that looked like an upside-down lightbulb, careful not to let any float away. They were fueled and ready to continue their journey.

"Cora?"

"Uh-huh?" She didn't take her eyes off the pathway.

"How do you get the submarines?"

"They are the one thing that we get from the human world. Then we add to them. Our own special touches." She winked.

*On land missions. Is purchasing a submarine one of the on-land missions?*

A mere hour later, they finally reached their destination, a dome-like building crafted out of mirrors. Claire chuckled to herself at the thought that the creator of the building had many years of bad luck. There were no indications of anyone occupying the area. It truly *appeared* to be abandoned.

"Welcome to headquarters!" Cora excitedly announced as they swam up to the eerie structure.

As Claire followed Cora, she noticed that the atmosphere seemed slightly different, less cheerful and welcoming. She could see in the mirrors that her hair was a wreck. Even in the water, she could tell it was a matted mess, not at all how she normally liked to look, certainly not presentable. She stroked her fingers through it, though it didn't do much. She should have used that hairbrush. There wasn't a single being around, and it was as silent as a library. *Maybe they are all inside of the peculiar structure, working?* Claire assumed and crossed her fingers. If they were *just* inside working, wouldn't she be able to hear them? Other than the swooshing sound they caused as they swam, silence fell upon them. Claire noticed then, in that new area they were in, that she had not yet seen a single fish or any sea life for that matter. The desolate territory reminded Claire of one of the post-apocalyptic towns in her little brother's zombie books that he was always jabbering about. The happy, colorful, lively merfolk world that she was used to had faded completely.

Had Claire just signed herself up for death? She hoped that it was more lively inside; otherwise, it would be quite depressing and further heighten her suspicion. However, when they entered, only one mer appeared inside. Claire could have sworn that she saw a shark out of the corner of her eye as they entered the building but remembered that Cora had told her there were none, so she shook off the idea.

A light flickered on the opposite side of the oddly large room. But would it even be a true office if there wasn't at least one light flickering? Claire had half expected to enter and see a mess of mers working away under blinding lights and was a bit weirded out as she scanned the oddly giant space. A beat-up, salvaged desk stretched across one unoccupied side and a few rusty file cabinets sat lonely in a corner.

"Welcome!" A single worker cheerfully shouted out.

Claire knew that she certainly wouldn't be that happy if she was the worker. Claire said hello, and then they continued on. Horrible thoughts started running through her mind. She could tell that she was sweating profusely even though she was immersed in water.

"Claire, are you alright?" Cora asked her.

"W—why is there only one worker?" Claire turned as white as a ghost.

"See, that's what there *seems* to be, but beneath the surface is so much more. This trick is just for security purposes. Quinn is one of the strongest female workers here! She's up here providing extra protection and to stall someone in case headquarters is ever broken into," Cora continued.

It all made sense to Claire after it had been explained. She prayed that it was the truth.

"Here, follow me. I'll show you where all the chaos is!"

*Beneath the surface.* She must have been hinting that there was an office underneath where they had been at that very moment. *Perhaps a hidden room?* At least, that was what Claire assumed. But where Coralia was leading her didn't seem to be anything other than a boring, old wall.

"Quinn, could you please activate the entrance?" Coralia politely asked the worker.

"Of course!" she exclaimed while unbuckling her seat belt. Down in the merfolk world, most chairs had a strap that mers could put across their tail to hold them onto their seat.

The female worker led Claire and Cora through a disguised doorway in the brick wall, a wall that ran across the very back of the room. That would seem to be all that there was to the structure, a wall that would certainly stall an intruder. Quinn then floated in front of a second wall that was hidden behind the disguised doorway they just came through, and Claire had no clue what she was doing. To her, it simply looked like a regular wall. *She knew it wasn't.* Claire's breath was taken away as she was sucked up into a tube which appeared out of nowhere. Before Claire could think twice, she, Cora, and Quinn were teleporting over the roof of the building and underground into the classified, secret workspace. It took barely half a second, like the portal that Coralia had taken her through earlier. Claire shook her head, trying to make sense of it all.

"Facial recognition and teleportation," Cora informed in a mysterious tone, knowing that Claire was confused by it and that it was a ton for her to take in all at once.

"What is facial recognition?" she asked, mouth agape.

"That's right, you don't have that in the human world yet, do you?"

Claire abruptly shook her head. *Are we supposed to get it?* Claire's head spun at how Cora knew so much and how the merfolk world was so extremely ahead of her world.

"All of the employees here are programmed into the system by a three-hundred-and-sixty-degree video of them along with tons of photos, and whenever one of those mers floats in that spot that we were just in, it detects them by that video, and the pictures. But first, they must get past Quinn!" Cora laughed while taking a glance at Quinn, who was smiling and holding back a laugh.

"So, if you are programmed into the system, you can bring someone down who doesn't work here?"

Coralia nodded slowly. "Yes, and well, that's a positive and a negative thing."

"Do you need anything else, Cora?"

"No, I don't believe so. But thank you, Quinn!"

Quinn nodded and teleported back to her private office.

"Wow! This is just . . ." Claire was surprised.

A room the size of a small market was full of mermaids and mermen working, thick walls of sand protecting them. That was a normal day for them. But for Claire, it was something completely out of the ordinary. Tons of screens, which looked to be old TVs with live feed of miscellaneous spots in the sea, were spread throughout the facility.

"What is all of this? I thought you said that this is just where they monitor that one area where planes can see in?"

"It's our monitoring area . . . for all the cameras. Or at least almost all of them" Cora pointed across the workspace. "See that very small peculiar-looking door over there?"

Claire nodded. The door was no larger than the average trap door.

"That's our monitoring and detecting room for that *exposed* area."

Claire thought for a moment, all of it not fully making sense to her. "But what's the reason for all these other cameras?"

"You see, we do our own research on fishermen, littering, and some other things too. Just like the people that are brought in on the planes, sometimes we bring fishermen in as well," Coralia explained.

Claire gave her a nod, processing it all. *Why though? Why do they bring in fishermen?* She was curious but didn't know if she should ask.

The screens for monitoring were the only source of light that far below the surface. Cora told Claire that the reasoning was so that every single detail on the screens could be seen clearly. She also told her that their workers got a quick break every hour so that their days at work wouldn't be so dark and depressing and something that wasn't enjoyable to them. But since someone had to always watch the screens, they took their breaks in separate groups. A few members lived there to monitor at night, as well. Besides, it was for their own good.

She peered throughout the room that she was now floating in, catching sight of one monitor that was streaming feed of a dock, then another one streaming from inside a boat, and one last monitor streaming from a camera that appeared to be in the middle of the dark, cloudy ocean. Several more monitoring screens hung across the walls of the workspace, some showing waters that all looked the same and some showing vastly different areas.

When they mentioned land missions, was *planting cameras* one of them? As Cora continued showing her around, Claire picked up that the mer workers were all in sync as they worked. *Interesting. Odd.* Cora proceeded to lead her into the small monitoring room. Only three monitoring screens hung on the wall in there. One camera appeared to be floating in the sky, one on a quite small island, in a swaying palm tree, and finally, the last one, floating in the water. They saw a plane on one of the monitors.

"Does that plane need to be brought in?" Claire asked, feeling helpful, right as a blaring alarm went off, which meant that it did indeed need to be brought in. Claire's hands flew to her ears. Boy, that was excruciatingly loud. "That's a yes, isn't it?" Claire laughed after it finally stopped, and so did Coralia while nodding.

Claire glanced back and noticed a tiny, box-shaped, glass room that a single mer happened to be sitting in. She hadn't even noticed the small, strange room when she had first entered the larger monitoring area that it was in. She assumed that it wouldn't hurt to question the reasoning for it. Therefore, she did.

"To protect the mer's eyes," Cora answered, very focused on the monitoring screens. "It's a rare, unique type of glass. The few minutes or so that we will be in here, touring, won't do damage to our eyes. However, when it's your job, and you are in here for between six and eight hours, all the unhealthy light will start to damage your eyes quickly," she added on, a slight frown pulling at her bottom lip.

Claire grimaced. "That . . . makes sense."

The worker inside the micro-monitoring box awkwardly waved at Claire.

"Is this what they do *all* day?"

"Indeed, for the most part, unless the day is extremely eventful. In that case, they would be swimming all over the place! It would be a mad house in here!"

*Eventful in what way?*

Claire had noticed that the mers working throughout the space had a floating, round, tinted shield over each eye, like sunglasses without frames. Every single worker. They were kind of freaky looking. She assumed they had a similar effect as the glass room the other worker had been in when she was touring—to protect their eyes.

"So, their day at work is fairly calm?" Claire questioned.

"You could say that!" Cora chuckled as Claire slowly swam around, studying the new area and screens very intensely.

*What are they **really** monitoring down here?*

# Clove

"**R**eady to go?" Roman asked Clove and Lucas as he buckled his seat belt.

Lucas quickly eyed Clove, who was sitting diagonally from him in the back seat. He looked concerned and so did Clove. While conversing about baseball, work, and old friends, Roman acted as if nothing had happened between him and Lucas.

Clove didn't say much, not wanting to accidentally aggravate her brother or spill his cruel secret. Luckily the ride was short and not too awkward. And Roman didn't drive them off a cliff, so they had to look on the bright side! Clove thought about how

Lucas would be able to drive soon. She liked the thought; she just wouldn't feel comfortable getting into a car with him until she was much older and he was a more experienced driver. She also knew that there was no way her parents would let her, either. Knowing thoughtful Lucas, he would offer her a ride to places whenever he got the chance. But she would worry about that and come up with some excuses when the time came.

*Enough thinking about it—about Lucas.*

She knew they were in the right place when they rolled into the parking lot for the tryouts. Cars filled the parking lot like a car dealership. Hundreds of high school guys were beginning to line up at the door of the castle-like school, while several were still warming up and stretching in the spruce tree-shaded areas. There were many girls, too, but the guys out numbered the girls by a sizable amount. Between the constant buzz of the cars zipping past on the highway, and the tons of teenagers chatting, it overwhelmed Clove's mind.

Clove walked ahead of her brother and Lucas. The crazy- bright sun glistened off the dozens of bikes on the side of the school. The glare hit Clove directly in the eye, blinding her for a few seconds, causing her to overstep and get her new shoe caught in a small crack in the pavement. Clove wasn't sure what embarrassing noise escaped her mouth without her approval, but she was sure it could be compared to the frightening sound of a howler monkey. Not quite a gasp but also not quite a scream.

Everyone gasped. She saw that most of the line of cars searching for empty spaces stopped moving except for the one car she was directly in front of.

Suddenly, she felt large, strong hands grip her waist, and with one swift movement, she was ripped away from extreme pain and possibly even . . . *death*. She landed on her side in the thick grass, a slight cushion under her. She coughed. The wind really hadn't been knocked out of her too badly. Anything was better than a parking-lot pavement death. But as she looked up and scanned around, the hero had already vanished. All she could see through her slight tunnel vision was some red hair whipping around in the crowd that was huddled in front of the main entrance. She was almost positive that she saw red hair out of the corner of her eye when the person grasped onto her. Was it him? And why did he run off so quickly? Ugh, and now she was the center of attention. *Wonderful!* People from all around started to rush toward her, trying to maneuver through the line of cars, shouting, and asking if she was okay.

"Hey!" Clove heard a girl bark out behind her after Lucas bumped into her.

"Move. I've got to get to her."

*Lucas*

"Ugh." By the bite in the girl's tone, Clove could tell that she was clearly very annoyed. For a moment Clove thought that the selfish Regina George herself was standing behind her.

Labored breaths got louder and louder and then she felt a warm hand on her back. "Are you okay?" Lucas's voice was soft and soothing. "Here, let me help you," he added before she even had a chance to formulate a sentence. He bent down and propped her back up against his leg, brushing her hair out of her face and picking off the bits of grass, leaves, and sticks that were stuck to her shirt.

"Are you alright, Clove?" Roman asked, finally getting up to them, practically falling to her side. His chest rose and fell as he breathed heavily. He looked terrified.

"Yeah. No worse than falling off my bike when I was little." She sort of laughed.

Roman had to be pretty mad that Lucas got to her first. She was just fine, though. She didn't land very hard at all but was a bit shaken up by the way her rescuer whipped her around and the fact that she was still alive.

"Are you okay? I am *so* sorry," said the girl who had been driving the car that almost ran Clove over. With fear written all over her face, she looked like she had seen a ghost.

Clove nodded, starting to get up. She could hear the girl let out a sigh of relief.

"Woah, take it easy," Roman said.

"I'm fine, really. And you guys need to get going." She could be stubborn sometimes.

Lucas quickly wiggled his arm under her armpits, and Roman put his hand around her back. She didn't need to become unconscious, fall, and crack her head open.

"Really, you guys, I'm fine." She laughed.

Everyone just gawked, dumbstruck, still in complete shock. It was *like* that person had some insane *powers*. Whoever it was got to her and swooped her up so fast. She had been a quarter of a second away from being as flat as a pancake on the pavement.

"Who was that that got me out of the way?" she asked, searching Roman's eyes.

"Jake Hall," Roman replied under his breath. "He's a humble guy; that's probably why he ran off so quickly."

Clove just had to find him to say thank you. With Roman on one side and Lucas on the other, they crossed the busy parking lot, checking for cars a bajillion times. They joined the crowd, tons of people asking Clove if she was okay. That was an incident that they certainly weren't going to tell Iris about. Oh no, what if another parent brought it up? Clove could only hope for the best. After squeezing their way through the crowd lined in front of the door, Lucas and Roman needed to go off for warm-ups.

"I really don't wanna leave you alone, Clove." Roman chewed on his lip, looking around as they stood in the rowdy hallway of the school.

"I. Will. Be. Fine." Clove nodded dramatically with each word she said.

He took a deep breath, letting it out slowly. "You need to come get me if—"

"Bye, Roman!" she called out as she spun around on her heel, waving.

Lucas looked nervous before she turned around, so she slowly glanced back over her shoulder, trying not to be too noticeable. Lucas was looking back, too, giving her a tender look. She just smiled. What would people say about him rushing to Clove's side? Obviously, he didn't care too much about what they had to say. And he would never just *let* something happen to her.

Clove finally found a seat—the ice-cold, hard bleachers. Judging by the crowd, a few parents, only a handful of siblings, and a few of what Clove assumed were girlfriends and boyfriends of the people trying out were staying to watch. She was surprised that baseball tryouts were being held indoors. As Clove scoped out the building, waiting for Lucas to make an appearance to flex his skills—*and biceps*—she saw giant nets hanging from the ceiling and a few alumni sitting at a table off to the side, ready to take notes. But when she looked up toward the balcony that overlooked the gym, she saw a shadowy figure standing there, who seemed to be unnoticed by most. She squinted against the buzzing lights overhead, attempting to stay unseen by the shady figure to see if she was actually seeing what she thought she was. And she definitely was. Her stomach knotted up. She found it odd that anyone would be up on the dark second story at that time, considering it was off-limits during tryouts. The figure finally moved, revealing himself as a janitor, which immediately calmed Clove's racing heart that was about to leap from her chest. She got spooked quite easily sometimes. But recently, she felt like she was always on high alert, like she was always full of caffeine. She didn't know why.

She looked around some more. She saw many people but hadn't spotted *Madelaine.* Tons of guys flooded the building, and she didn't see one with looks that beat Lucas's stunning appearance. Then the text crept into her mind. Ugh, those words. She just wanted to forget about them already. And luckily, she had been successful at keeping it a secret and not slipping up. A *deep*, dark secret.

Clove peered throughout the ginormous room, still not spotting her brother or Lucas. She wished that she would have asked what time they were starting.

As the coach yelled out and waved kids in, they made their appearance at last. Lucas and Roman came out in different lines and as they did, her eyes focused in on a dim corner. Her mind transported again to a flashback; Coralia and Claire entered the hidden tunnel system—the bustling underground world. Clove found it surreal with all its shops and restaurants and mysterious, tucked away curiosities. It was certainly something out of the ordinary. What Clove did see, though, was Hudson pushing his way through the heavy crowd, trying to get to Claire as quickly as possible, all while carrying a bunch of seaweed in his arms. When Claire was preoccupied and ran into Hudson, excitement surged through Clove's body at their meeting once more. It was a mere vision in her mind, but still, she was excited for Claire.

"Lucas Lynch and Roman Riley," a coach called the boys up to try out, swiftly breaking off Clove's flashback.

She popped her head up, searching for Lucas. Someone next to her gave her a funny look and raised her eyebrows at Clove.

Clove bent over slightly, holding her stomach. "Sorry, cramps!" She giggled nervously at her stupid excuse for her odd behavior of staring off into nowhere and, well, for whatever else her body did without her approval while the flashback took control. If she told her the truth, she would get wheeled out of there on a stretcher and taken to a mental facility.

The girl just nodded, and Clove looked away quickly. She didn't have a single clue as to what would get Lucas and Roman on the team or what would prevent them from making it. Still, she watched, eager to hopefully congratulate them at the end. There was no sign of her brother which worried her, considering that he was supposed to go up at the same time as Lucas. *Where did he go? They came out together right before the flashback started,* she remembered.

She didn't know if she could get up and walk around, but she didn't care. She proceeded down the bleachers closer to where Lucas was, waited until it appeared as if he was finished with his try-out, which he seemed to have aced, then headed out of the gym to try to find her brother.

"Sorry, Miss, this area is off-limits to you."

Clove scrunched up her face and raised an eyebrow, trying to think of something to say that would make the coach let her in. "Oh? Why is that?" she asked, stalling.

"Only high schoolers."

"So, you just assumed I'm not one? I'm sorry that I'm short."

He pressed his lips together in a straight line, irritated. "Well then, in that case, are you a girlfriend of someone? A sis—"

She cut him off before he could finish. She probably should have waited two more seconds until he asked her if she was a sister of someone. She could have simply said that she was Roman's sister, but she was just too dang impatient to wait for him to finish his sentence. "Yes, a girlfriend," she lied, but she just had to know why her brother hadn't appeared for his tryout—if he was okay—*what* he was doing.

"I see. And who would that be?"

"Lucas . . ." she said. "Lucas Lynch!" She needed to sound believable since her looks certainly didn't help.

The coach raised an eyebrow as he glanced down at his clipboard. "Two left turns, then it'll be the fifth door on the right. And my apologies for the mix-up." He flashed a quick, unconvincing smile, happy to see her leave and not be his problem anymore.

*Well, that was easy*, she thought, trying to suppress her mischievous smirk. Now she would have to tell Lucas that she convinced the coach she was his girlfriend. *Wonderful.* It may have been a wish, though it certainly wasn't true. As she passed through the hallways, her imagination messing with her, she pushed her way closer to that fifth door through muscular, sweaty, teen guys. Most didn't even acknowledge her.

At last, there was a clearing, right at the perfect spot too, the *fifth* door! She stopped and knocked. She heard tons of people chatting. It was very noisy in there. Had anyone even heard her knocking? The door quickly whipped open; a guy who had to be no more than her brother's age stood in the doorway. He ran a hand through his flame-colored hair. Boy was he tall—The Statue of Liberty tall. At first, Clove was distracted by his six-pack, then realized he may be the guy who saved her from falling into traffic. She gasped. She got her wish. She found him.

"Hey, you caught me, didn't you?"

He smiled. "I did."

"Well, I—I really can't thank you enough!"

"Ah, no problem! You alright?"

A soft smile spread across Clove's face, and she nodded, blushing slightly. If it weren't for him, Clove might've—would have gotten run over. "Is . . . um . . . Lucas here?"

He nodded. "Sure thing, c'mon in! Lucas, you've got a visitor!" Clove's six-pack rescuer called out.

*What is this place?* Packed bookshelves took up lots of the wall space, and a giant TV stretched across almost half a wall with a very comfy-looking couch directly across. It looked like some luxury school hangout. The room had to be at least the size of three normal classrooms. It was way nicer than any school hangout Clove had ever been in.

"Clove, hey." Lucas seemed slightly surprised that she was his visitor as he flew around the corner. He looked worried, but she threw a reassuring smile his way.

There had to be at least fifty guys packed into the room. Clove didn't know where to go to talk to Lucas in private or if that was even possible. Stepping out into the hallway wouldn't work because it had just as many people as the hangout area, if not more.

"You okay?" He raised his eyebrows and searched her eyes.

"Yeah. But I need to talk to you for a second," she told him.

Lucas bit his lip while scratching his head, unsure where to go. "Well . . . uh . . . follow me."

Clove got a few odd looks as she walked through the large room to a small terrace overlooking a quickly streaming river, taking the falling leaves with it. It was gorgeous. And not a single person was outside, so it was perfect.

"After you."

Clove gave Lucas a polite smile at his kind gesture.

"What's up?"

Clove looked around nervously and gulped. *Don't slip up.* "First, have you seen my brother?"

Lucas shook his head. "I wish. I haven't seen him since we were in line for tryouts. I swear I looked away for two seconds, and he was gone. It's not like him to just . . . bail."

Like Lucas, Clove shook her head, confused and frustrated. "Also—" Clove held her breath for a second.

Lucas looked down, directly into her eyes. "Also, what?"

"I told one of the coaches I'm your girlfriend so I could get back here, so . . ." her voice trailed off, her heart racing like crazy. Her palms grew more clammy with each word she said.

"I—okay. That's fine. You did what you needed to do. Thanks for letting me know." He didn't seem the least bit upset.

She nodded and let out a breath of relief. *What does that mean? Probably nothing, right?* He couldn't change what she told the coach, so why get upset? It wasn't really a big deal, anyway.

"Just, if we pass him, stay close to me so he will hopefully buy the lie."

Clove nodded. That certainly wouldn't be hard for her. "Any idea of where Roman might possibly be?"

"The other hangout area. It's not very popular. Normally, he and a few other people are in there."

"Where is it?"

"All the way in the back of the school. You'll never find it if I just tell you how to get there." Lucas glanced at his watch. "But you know what, I can't exactly leave right now." He thought momentarily, then stepped back inside, searching the room. "Jake, could you take her to the other hangout area?"

"The one on the other side of the school?" Jake laughed, but he did agree. "Sure."

Clove smiled as Mr. Abs walked over.

"Are you Lucas's girl—"

"Oh, no, no! But if any coaches ask, I am. That's how I got back here." She laughed nervously. "So please—"

"I won't say a thing. Who are you looking for, anyway?"

"My brother, Roman Riley. Do you know him?"

"I do."

Clove smiled. "Have you *seen* him?"

Jake shook his head.

As they got to the far side of the school, it got very quiet, and the crowd thinned out. The air was thick and smelled musty, reminding Clove of a horror movie. She could see why her brother liked it.

"Now, do you know Lucas very well?"

"A little better than I know your brother." Jake seemed to be very nice.

Suddenly, he halted at a dark, dingy door which had a frame that was in need of repair. "Well, this is it." Jake gestured to the door.

Clove looked inside, and at first, she didn't see a soul. But when she looked again, she spotted her brother sitting in there with a doll-like girl. They were much closer to each other than Clove preferred to see them. The girl's raven-black and pencil-straight hair was so long it piled in her lap. She was smiling, laughing, and staring into Roman's eyes like what they were doing was perfectly okay.

Clove gasped, throwing a hand over her gaping mouth, and quickly hid behind the wall beside the door. "Do you know who that girl is?"

From the side, she looked *just like* Lucas's girlfriend.

"I don't know her well, but . . ." He acted as if he wasn't sure if he should tell Clove what he was about to say. "Last I heard, that was um . . . Lucas's girlfriend . . ." He paused again, thinking. "Actually, I think that they may have broken up, though not that long ago. I'm really not sure."

"He can't see us here, especially me," Clove said in a hushed tone, panicked.

They both rushed around the corner, practically on their tiptoes, Clove not exactly knowing what to think. She knew they may have been dating but didn't want to believe it. Though seeing them like that *confirmed* it.

"How—how long ago did you hear they broke up?"

"I'd say . . . no more than two weeks ago."

"Look, this has to stay between us. Only us." She huffed. "I can't have my brother knowing that I saw him and whoever she is together," Clove said while swinging her hand up in the air, motioning toward the room that her brother and the girl were in. "And I certainly can't break that news to Lucas quite yet, not after how much of a jerk my brother has been to him lately. So please, keep this to yourself."

"I understand. No problem," Jake answered as they jogged through the hallways.

Could she trust Jake?

"Crap, what should I tell Lucas?" Clove shook her head in confusion.

"I hate to say this, but . . . lie, I guess."

*She had heard very similar words before.*

"Say that nobody was in there. Or at least say that Roman wasn't. Lucas probably won't believe you if you say that no one at all was in there."

"That's true," she said. He had a good point. "They probably aren't dating anymore, because my brother wouldn't . . ." her voice trailed off at that thought. She couldn't be so sure. Maybe she *didn't know* him as *well* as *she thought.*

"I'm not sure. They are—" he stopped himself suddenly, knowing he had already said too much.

"What? They are what?"

"Uh, never mind." Jake got weird.

Just as she was going to start to speak, they returned to the giant area where tryouts were being held. Coaches were shouting names and piercing sounds of whistles were echoing off the walls.

There, her desperate question sat unanswered.

Jake looked down at his watch and grimaced. "Do you think you could manage to get back to the room that Lucas is in by yourself?"

"Oh, yes, of course. Thank you for taking me over there! Not that I exactly love what I saw!" Clove smiled awkwardly.

"Same," Jake answered, stretching his calf.

"Oh, and thank you again for saving me!"

Jake looked up. "Anytime!" He smiled and half-laughed.

Clove walked beside the bleachers, absolutely hating the thought of lying to Lucas. Technically, she didn't have to, but she just couldn't break the news to him . . . yet. Or perhaps they *were* broken up, he knew that they were dating, and Clove was simply blowing it out of proportion?

"Well then, where could he be?" Lucas paced back and forth in front of Clove.

"If only I knew," Clove whispered under her breath, hoping to not sound suspicious. "How much longer do you have to stay, anyway?"

"I can leave anytime; I'm just waiting on Roman." He half-laughed, annoyed.

"Did you try texting him?"

"About twenty minutes ago."

Clove sighed. Now she had the perfect opportunity for one of her nosy questions. "Shouldn't your girlfriend be here?"

"Yeah, actually. I don't know where she is at the moment." He acted genuine.

*Are they still together? Or are they not?*

Lucas gestured for Clove to follow him back into the hangout room from the terrace.

"Well, feel free to make yourself at home. We might be here for a while!"

Clove seated herself in a small, antique-looking chair that sat under a fake tree in a corner with a skylight, which would have been the *perfect* spot for reading. She wished she had a book. If only she would have remembered about the shelves and shelves of books just around the corner. But her mind was too boggled to remember that. She knew that eventually her brother would show up. Considering that Clove knew where he was, she wasn't too worried about him. Her concern about the rest of the situation was a whole different story.

After several minutes of plain and simple sitting in the chair, watching the clouds shift in form through the skylight, she heard the hangout room door creak, and she hopped up, very hopeful that it was her brother. Instead, it was another familiar face, Jake, Mr. Abs.

"How'd your tryout go?" Clove kindly asked Jake.

"I think pretty well, but who knows." He shrugged.

"Come on, you were our captain. You couldn't have been complete crap! Don't be so hard on yourself!" a random guy in the room called out jokingly, and Jake laughed.

Clove had no clue that he had previously been captain, but she should have known, with his strapping build and charm. *Don't all captains look like that?*

He slowly went over to Clove, who had sat back down by then. "Have you seen him yet?"

"No. You?"

Jake shook his head as an irritated expression washed over Clove's face.

*Suddenly, she had an idea.* She didn't know why she hadn't thought of it earlier. "Where's Lucas? Do you know?"

"He should be right through that door."

"Okay. Thanks!" Clove eagerly popped up, even quicker than before.

"Lucas, you've got my mom's number, correct? I forgot my phone, but—"

He raised an eyebrow. "I think so. Why, Clove?" he asked suspiciously.

"She won't be too happy to hear that Roman isn't watching over me. Maybe she wouldn't mind giving us a ride home." A sinister smile took over Clove's face, then spread to Lucas's.

"Hey, Iris?" He paused for a moment, listening. "Yes, we are still at tryouts and cannot find Roman. Um . . . we are wondering if you can give us a ride home?" He asked, a blank stare upon his face, somewhat patiently waiting for a response. "Okay, we will head outside in a few. Thanks."

Clove's parents certainly wouldn't be too happy, but if Roman was dating Lucas's girlfriend, he deserved the consequences.

"I just don't get it. What happened to him? It's like he's a completely different person nowadays," Lucas shared his thought with Clove as they stood outside, waiting for Clove's mother.

She shook her head. "I—I don't know." She didn't want to say too much and spill the beans.

"So, your birthday is coming up soon, huh?" Lucas smirked, meeting her eyes.

She grinned while her porcelain-like cheeks turned a light shade of red. "I am *so* excited. I can't believe it's only ten days away!"

"Are you doing any big party or anything?"

"I've finally decided and invited a few friends to go go-karting!" She held her breath for a moment, having a speedy, nervous debate on whether she should or shouldn't say what she was about to.

"Oh, that's cool."

"I'd like you to come too."

Lucas turned his head toward Clove. "Me? Really?"

"Mhm," Clove mumbled.

"That's awfully nice. Thanks for the invite. I'll be there!" He smiled big.

Clove had been so nervous about inviting Lucas, but there it was, it finally came out. She didn't even know why she had been so nervous; she just was.

Clove suddenly went into a gaze. She thought she was going to black out. She could hear Lucas saying something to her, but it was as if she could not speak. *Another flashback.* Claire and Hudson simply sharing a stare and then Hudson swimming away. Coralia told Claire that she thought Hudson was fond of her. Claire turned as red as a child being embarrassed by their parent. After swimming off, Claire hadn't realized that Hudson had been looking back at her almost the whole time while she faded into the crowd. She highly doubted that a guy would ever like her for the right reasons. The only reason guys had ever even thought about liking her was to get back at a previous girlfriend.

*How am I experiencing Claire's thoughts?*

Again, Claire missed the so-called ghost mer. As the transporter's doors latched closed, the ghost mer swam up. It didn't seem as if anyone else noticed it, either.

Upon the entrance into Coralia's home using her perplexing nail key, the flashback became slightly fuzzy, as if Clove was being pulled in and out of it.

"Clove?" Lucas urged, his voice becoming clearer than before, but Clove still had difficulty transitioning back to reality. It was like she knew she needed to but physically couldn't. Lucas pinched the back of her arm, attempting to get her attention discreetly while he sat next to her on a hard metal bench. He was genuinely very worried.

"Ow!" Clove snapped her head his way, narrowing her eyes at him.

"Your mom is here."

Clove's heart started racing again for about the tenth time that day, and she searched the area, her eyes now wide, realizing that her mother was far enough away not to notice. She immediately relaxed.

"I've been trying to get you to snap out of that flashback since she pulled into the parking lot. It took a while," Lucas let the words escape from the corner of his mouth.

Clove shook her head. "Sorry. There was another strange—very strange part."

Clove's mother pulled up so close that she was practically touching the curb. "Do you know where your brother could be inside that school?" Iris asked as they pulled out of the parking lot onto the main road, wracking her brain.

"No, I—we don't, really." She shot a glance at Lucas then looked back at her mother.

Clove absolutely despised lying. She felt as if she was breaking the law. Should she tell her mother that she saw him when they could speak in private? "Did you try to call him?" Clove asked her mother. It was quite obvious that Iris heard her, but it was as if she was ignoring her. "Mom!"

"Sorry, I thought that you were talking to Lucas."

"No, no, I wasn't. I was staring straight at you."

Lucas chuckled under his breath. Watching and listening to a conversation between Clove and her mother was like watching a live comedy show sometimes.

"And yes, I did. I didn't get anything other than his voicemail." By her mother's tone alone, Clove could tell she was vexed.

Clove shook her head, very irritated and frustrated with her brother. After all, she had sort of believed that he had changed, but he was literally just trying to buy her forgiveness and trust, wasn't he?

After dinner that evening, Clove heard the front door make a high-pitched squeak. It was nearly eleven. Along with the squeak, her brother cursed. Obviously, he was trying to not be heard or seen, but Clove wasn't going to let that happen. She had been sitting in his room for over an hour, waiting for him to arrive home so that she could give him an earful after her parents were done with him. While she waited, she perched herself on his bed, remembering how much more comfortable his bed was than her own.

Clove had a feeling that she would give Roman a slight heart attack when he switched the light on and had the pleasant surprise of her presence in his room. If this incident didn't make her parents regret letting him get his license so early, she didn't know what would. It was a shame, too, because normally, he was a good-choice-making, responsible, caring son, brother, and friend, but lately, he was a complete jerk. It was as if he wasn't even anywhere near the same person Clove had known her entire life. She really hoped that he wouldn't shower because she was determined to question him, but gosh, was she tired.

Once she heard footsteps on the stairs, she barely took a breath. Her heart started to pound as he got closer and closer to entering his room. Could he hear it? Heck, the whole block probably could. The footsteps stopped. Ugh, he stopped to use the bathroom. She rolled her eyes and sighed. *Really?* She laughed to herself, trying not to give herself away. She really didn't know what was so funny. What was so funny was how delusional she was from staying up and being tired. That was probably why everything was hilarious. Finally, he came out, walked over to his room, flicked the light on, and like Clove suspected, got quite the scare. He gasped and just about threw his heavy-duty water bottle at her, which would have knocked her out cold.

"God Clove, why *must* you be in here?" Roman asked through clenched teeth, narrowing his eyes at her. Then he went about his business, taking his uniform top off and throwing on something more comfortable.

"Where were you?" Clove asked, not giving him any time before tacking more on. "You know, lately, I don't even feel like you're my brother anymore. What—what if I really would have needed to find you today at the school? Lately, it's been Lucas who has been there for me. Not you. It's like you completely changed personalities with someone, and certainly not for the good." Clove yawned. She probably shouldn't have mentioned Lucas, but she didn't even care right then.

He flashed a furious glare her way, but then he pondered for a moment, not thrilled by her statement, but he knew it was the truth; he just didn't want to admit it.

"Also, why didn't you try out? Where were you when you were nowhere to be found? Because I came loo—"

"You can't tell anyone, okay, not even Lucas." He rubbed his forehead, gazing into the distance. "Hear me?"

She still needed to play stupid, though. She moved to the edge of the bed and searched his eyes, acting as if she was eager for an answer. She sort of was, in a way. Was he going to lie?

"And I'm sorry, okay? I really am. I've got a new girlfriend, and we were hanging out before tryouts. I . . . lost track of time. And where was I tonight? I lost track of time again, then I panicked, drove way over the speed limit, and . . . got a ticket."

Clove's jaw dropped. She wanted to laugh. "A ticket!" she yelled out much louder than necessary.

His story didn't completely make sense. Clove definitely saw him come out in the lineup for tryouts. What happened in those two seconds that no one saw him disappear? He just had the urge to be with Madelaine and ran off all of a sudden? Why would he throw his chance to try out down the drain? That wasn't at all characteristic of him. Madelaine must be one heck of a girl.

"Jeez, could you be just a little louder? It's not like I really *wanted* to tell Mom and Dad."

"Sorry. Just . . . who's this new girl?" Clove asked a little too excitedly.

He took a long, deep breath. Was he trying to think of a lie to feed Clove?

"Lucas's ex-girlfriend." Roman stared down at his hands as if he were ashamed.

Clove could very well tell he knew what he was doing was messed up.

"Were you two dating when they—"

"Clove, come on, I'll admit, sure, I've been a jerk lately, but dating my best friend's girlfriend when they were still dating—I would never betray Lucas like that. *Ever.*"

*Like dating your best friend's ex-girlfriend is much better?*

Clove didn't completely believe him, not yet anyway, especially with how he had been acting lately. "How long?"

"Two months." Roman tensed his jaw as if he wasn't positive on his word.

"So, Lucas doesn't know? Doesn't suspect it?"

"Oh, God, no. I mean . . . I don't think so. And absolutely do not tell him Clove. Get it? Do. Not. Tell. Him." He had a fiery gaze in his eyes.

# *Claire*

Upon leaving the place of monitoring, Coralia struck up a conversation informing Claire that if she got the tail treatment to become half-mer, she would slowly adjust to needing less sleep. Claire smiled. Having more hours to work or do what she adored sounded terrific to her. But what about all the extra baggage that came along with the decision to stay there and receive the tail treatment? Claire still wasn't so sure she could look past all of that. *She still wasn't sure she could pass up the opportunity either.* It was insane. In some ways, she wished that it was all simply a dream so she could wake up in her own house, her own bed, surrounded by her family, and her worries and extremely tough decisions she needed to make would be non-existent. At the exact same time, she prayed it was all real.

In the evening, after the tour had been dragged out and ended up taking practically the entire day, Claire had been running through her thoughts once more when a very light knock sounded on her giant suite door, one that sounded as if a child had barely tapped their finger on it.

Her heart nearly jumped a beat when she glanced through the tiny peep hole in the door. She quickly ripped it open. "Hudson!" she exclaimed, taking a quick glance down to see a bundle of flowers in his hands, confused for a moment as to why he was there. He looked so handsome. Claire thought his dazzling eyes looked particularly alluring that night and his bronzed skin emphasized the definition of his physique in a way she hadn't noticed before.

"Hi . . ." He paused. "I'm sorry, I was debating for a while whether I should come over, but then I figured I'd just stop by. I thought, what's the worst that could happen? She won't answer?" He laughed nervously, running a trembling hand through his hair.

She tried not to make it too obvious that she liked him, but it grew more difficult to pretend she didn't. Claire didn't waste a second to answer. "Oh, but I'm so glad that you did! Would you like to come in for a few?" She bit her lip, praying he would say yes.

He nodded, and a giant, unmistakable grin spread across Claire's face. When Hudson proceeded forward through the doorway, he immediately lost his tail, and his legs appeared. His shaggy hair went from dark brown to a slicked back dirty blonde as Claire assumed it would. He wore a pair of beige shorts, and a deep navy-blue shirt that complimented his eyes so well. His cologne floated off him, and she thought the scent was so nice; it was a scent that wasn't familiar to her. She wondered if the merfolk made it. It was certainly different. They both made their way to the living room area and sat.

"Oh, these are for you!" He smiled big while handing the beautiful flower bouquet to Claire. He seemed just as giddy and excited to give the flowers to her as she was to receive them. She smiled back at Hudson like a fool in love, but Claire was taken aback when his eyes met hers. There was a sense of determination in his gaze.

"Awe, thank you so much! These are—wow, this is so sweet!" A bundle of purple and yellow sea flowers held together with a bit of colored fishing line. They didn't resemble anything Claire had seen before; they were pretty, though.

"What a relief! I had not a single idea of what color to bring you." He also seemed nervous and jittery, shifting in his seat often.

"I like any color, but these, these are gorgeous!" She leaned over and smelled them. "Oh, and they have a delightful scent too!" Claire had completely forgotten to worry if they were human-friendly or not. But he wouldn't give her poisonous flowers, right? *Not unless that was their evil scheme—save the innocent human girls, have a charming merman bring them poisonous flowers, then boom, they're dead.*

Claire briefly thought about how she hadn't crossed paths with any other humans down there. But the flowers weren't dissolving her yet, so she was most likely safe. Claire felt as if Hudson wanted to say something but wasn't sure how to get the words out—as if he was searching for the perfect way and time to say what he was hoping to. She was growing more and more anxious as the clock ticked by, even though only a few moments had passed. But she needed to be patient. Great things came with time.

"How are you able to simply just walk in here? Coralia couldn't even come in." Claire made conversation as she searched his eyes.

"She and I use different magic."

Claire nodded in the moment of silence. She found all of it quite intriguing.

"I know that it's sort of strange, me stopping by like this. I just have to ask you something; I can't wait any longer."

*He needed to get it over with already.*

Her intuition was right. Her lips started to curl up in a smile, and her eyebrows rose high.

"First, I—I would like to apologize for how I was this morning. I was not a gentleman at all, and I am really, truly sorry. I hope you can forgive me for that."

Cora said that he was like that with everyone when he first met them. Was that true?

Quickly, Claire nodded. She'd at least give him a chance. He seemed decent enough. "Of course! I was quite demanding myself, you know!"

Hudson smirked slightly as he laughed. He held Claire's gaze for a moment then looked away. *If only Claire knew how much he already liked her too.* "I know this is a long shot, but . . . are you going to live here?" he asked.

That was certainly a tough question that required much reflection. "Maybe," she said.

"Just maybe?"

How could he expect her to have a definite answer to that question so soon?

She still didn't want to get anyone's hopes up too high. Especially her own. Truly, she didn't know what she should do or what she was going to do. And the clock was ticking.

"If I recall, you're around my age, correct?" Hudson asked.

"Well, I'm . . ." She didn't want to say it, because, well, how old was he exactly? She didn't want her age to be a turn off for him. "I'm sixteen." Clove held her breath while waiting for him to say something—anything.

"Well then, yeah, we're—we're close in age."

Why didn't he tell her his age? Why did it seem like such a secret?

He took a deep breath. "Claire, could I take you on a date tomorrow evening?" he blurted out, unable to hold it in a minute longer.

Claire's jaw dropped at his words. "Yes, yes, absolutely, of course!" She giggled in shock, since she had never had a fella interested in her. She could feel her heart fluttering in her chest.

"Perfect." Hudson nodded as he thought of something to say. He shifted in his seat, fiddling his hands. "What time is good for—"

"Any!" Claire answered, cutting him off from finishing his sentence.

"Well then, perhaps I could pick you up at five-thirty? Also, the destination that I've been planning on taking you to is around an hour's time away. Is that okay with you? I can find somewhere else—"

"No, please don't. That sounds ... perfect!" Claire interrupted him again, noticing that he seemed to be getting flustered. "Absolutely perfect!" Claire's small smile bloomed like a flower in spring. He had been *planning*?

"Great! I'll let you get to bed, though. It's getting late." Hudson got to the door when he remembered to ask Claire, "Do you have a phone in here? You've got to."

She looked confused. "A phone? I haven't yet seen one."

Hudson stepped over to the minuscule cabinet that held such a gorgeously crafted, unique lamp, dropped to his knees, and got it open after pulling with much force, revealing a fancy phone that didn't look like it had been used a single time. "Ah-ha! Do you mind if I get the number on the bottom, just in case something was to happen, and I couldn't get over here to cancel in person?" He slowly pulled a long, pointy shell out of his pocket.

"No, I don't mind at all. That would be very good, actually."

Hudson quickly jotted down the number on his hand, and it disappeared into his skin. "Have a delightful evening, Claire!" He gave her a soft smile.

She smiled back as he turned around. Claire could hardly wrap her head around what had just happened. She really didn't believe it at all. "Good night to you too!"

While turning, he gave Claire a wink that caused her to erupt in goose bumps. She felt like fireworks were exploding in her stomach.

"Thank you for the flowers!" she called out at last. Although it could not be heard, she was screaming at the top of her lungs inside. *Where is he taking me?* She hadn't asked him because she liked surprises. Good surprises, that was. *What do I wear?* After a few moments of pondering, she remembered the enchanted chest's ability to supply clothing!

Claire tossed and turned half the night. *She agreed to go on a date with a merman, a fantastical being?!* She was restless and exhilarated about her first upcoming date and thinking about her family and Maggie and how much she missed them. They must have been terrified. Those thoughts made her decision terribly difficult. Then finally, her racing mind became exhausted enough, and she fell into a deep sleep.

However, that didn't last long. She found herself being awoken an hour or so later by the similar sound which had interrupted her rest the night prior, but this time, it was blood-curdling. She had practically jumped out of her skin at its shrill tone. Like the day before, she attempted to fall back asleep, assuming it was a similar event that was taking place.

As the commotion grew louder and louder and Claire couldn't fall back to what had been her peaceful rest, she decided to look out the window, not sure if she even wanted to know what was happening. She saw many mers, including Coralia, rushing about in a frantic manner. Claire's heart rate picked up a bit. At that moment, Claire knew that a horrific event had occurred by the expressions on their faces. Their expressions—full of longing and despair and confusion—were devastating to Claire. Some floated about looking simply mindless.

Claire didn't know exactly what had occurred. The one thing that she could most definitely tell was that it wasn't at all good. Was it safe or not for her to leave her room? Wouldn't they have already warned her if it wasn't? Perhaps they just hadn't had the time yet? Maybe it happened within the last few minutes, considering it had just woken her.

Claire paced the room for a few minutes, contemplating if she should put her own life in danger just to know what happened. Or, she could wait in the comfort of the suite, possibly still in danger of what was out there—*who* was out there.

*No, she wasn't going to just wait.* She practically soared through the water to get to the main door that would allow her to exit the building. She'd never swam so fast in her whole entire life. It was as if some sort of force propelled her. Since Claire was swimming at lightning speed, she got quite the goose egg when she smashed into the locked main door, which, to her knowledge, had always been unlocked before.

Perhaps it automatically locked when there was a dangerous or murderous affair in order?

"Ow!" Claire cried out while rapidly seizing her forehead.

Claire looked around helplessly. There was no one to help her get out. Maybe she really was locked in there for a valid reason. But that certainly didn't mean that she liked the fact. Honestly, she truly despised it, even knowing that it was most likely for her own good. She wasn't going to give up. Not now, *not ever*. She began forcefully pounding on the main door, attempting to draw as much attention as achievable. It was as if no one was able to hear her. Or maybe they were just completely ignoring her. Considering all the chaos, perhaps they actually *couldn't* hear her?

She kept pounding on the door, more harshly and powerfully each time, as if her life depended on it.

*Nobody came.*

Despite the chaos of the moment, she still wondered, *am I dreaming?*

**WHAT HAS HAPPENED TO CAUSE SUCH CHAOS
IN THE MERFOLK WORLD?**

Does Claire decide to stay or return to her family?
The flashbacks have brought Clove and Lucas
closer together—will that spark between them
finally catch fire?
More secrets.
More danger.
A bond that might finally become something more.

You've only scratched the surface . . .
of the flashbacks . . . of the truth.
The real story awaits you.
Don't miss book two . . . coming soon.

Stay intrigued at www.sirihutton.com
For sneak peeks, release dates,
and exclusive extras.

# About The Author

This gal is a free-spirited, Florida-based author. Siri is a proud dog mom and an avid tennis player. No matter what Siri is doing, she is normally listening to an audiobook, assessing it for her mobile bookshop or jamming out to her favorite tunes, cluelessly dancing about the house. She has always cherished writing, but recently decided that life is too short to not start pursuing her dreams now, especially her dream of publishing fun, sweet novels. Her mother was truly the first person who got her hooked on writing, by buying her little DIY books that she designed when she was very young.

Before anyone could blink, she went from the little girl scribbling fantasy stories to the young lady publishing them.

Siri's newsletter that follows her life of being an indie author is a fun and often humorous read, and she would love for you to join the exclusivity of her newsletter family where you will receive updates on future book releases.

www.sirihutton.com

She also adores hanging out on her socials and looks forward to interacting with you on them!

**f**

Siri Hutton's Series

instagram.com/author.siri.hutton/

g

goodreads.com/sirihutton

If you loved this story as much as Siri loved writing it, a positive review would be highly appreciated!

www.ingramcontent.com/pod-product-compliance
Lightning Source LLC
Chambersburg PA
CBHW061223310726

48971CB00007B/1919